Nigel West, the ~~~~~~~~~~~~~~~~~~~~~~~~~~~~~
Quarterly, has written a number of non-fiction works
on the subject of security and espionage. He was
voted 'The Expert's Expert' by the *Observer* and is
an acknowledged authority in his field. In writing
Murder In The Commons, he has drawn on his
experience as a police officer in Westminster and as
a government back-bencher.

Critical acclaim for Nigel West:

'West's cracking expertise rivals Len Deighton's'
Observer

'Nigel West is generally much better than any other
spy writer' *Evening Standard*

'Urbane, reasonable, convincing' *The Economist*

Also by Nigel West

Non fiction

Spy! (*with Richard Deacon*)
MI5: British Security Service Operations, 1909–45
MI6: British Secret Intelligence Service Operations,
1909–45
A Matter of Trust: MI5, 1945–72
Unreliable Witness: Espionage Myths of World War II
The Branch: A History of the Metropolitan Police
Special Branch
GARBO (*with Juan Pujol*)
GCHQ: The Secret Wireless War
Molehunt
The Friends: Britain's Postwar Secret Intelligence
Operations
Games of Intelligence
Seven Spies Who Changed the World
Secret War: The Story of SOE

Fiction

The Blue List
Cuban Bluff

Murder In The Commons

Nigel West

HEADLINE

Copyright © 1992 Westintel Research Ltd

The right of Nigel West to be identified as the Author of
the Work has been asserted by him in accordance with the
Copyright, Designs and Patents Act 1988.

First published in 1992
by Macmillan London Limited

First published in paperback in 1993
by HEADLINE BOOK PUBLISHING PLC

10 9 8 7 6 5 4 3 2 1

ISBN 0 7472 4176 7

Phototypeset by Intype, London

Printed and bound in Great Britain by
HarperCollins Manufacturing, Glasgow

HEADLINE BOOK PUBLISHING PLC
Headline House
79 Great Titchfield Street
London W1P 7FN

Contents

Murder In
The Commons

Prologue

The Honourable Member

The division had been called three minutes ago, and the Members' Lobby was a throng of men and women heading for the chamber. All were pressing to enter one of the two division lobbies before the Speaker ordered the doors locked after the required eight minutes. This was the one occasion when the press were excluded from the Members' Lobby, so the only people present were the smartly dressed doorkeepers, instantly identifiable in their white ties and tails, with their solid silver badges of office, and the uniformed policemen. Each had one eye on the library corridor to keep the lobby correspondents out of the way of the Members on their way to vote, and the other on the gallery doorways to stop the public who had obtained tickets to the various special galleries overlooking the chamber from entering the lobby. The doorkeepers, known since 1547 as Badge Messengers, slipped in and out of the milling crowd, passing telephone messages on pink slips of paper and envelopes from the

1

pigeonholes in the letter-board.

It was a regular ten o'clock division, but as it was a Thursday night the atmosphere was rather different to the rest of the week. Most Scottish Members were anxious to catch the 10.40 night train to Edinburgh from King's Cross, so their briefcases were piled up close to the exit, ready for a quick getaway. The ordered taxis had already gathered under the canopy in New Palace Yard, waiting for their fares.

Some MPs congregated in the lobby exchanging gossip in anticipation of their pairs emerging from the division. Was there to be just one vote, or was there a tedious amendment that might delay the departures? Might there be another division later? Or perhaps even an organised ambush on the government at the end of the Money Resolution – this was the extraordinary ritual where the conventional secrecy surrounding each party's voting intentions for the following week was compromised by Members telling their pairs what had been decided by the whips and disclosed to the parliamentary party at the weekly meeting held every Thursday at six o'clock. Having hastily exchanged notes those MPs blessed with pairs headed to their respective whips' clerks to register their absences during particular votes the following week.

Not all MPs were anxious to be away immediately after the division. Some might have a contribution to make in one of the less contentious debates scheduled for discussion later in the evening, and there was always a backbencher, selected by ballot, to close the day's proceedings with the adjournment debate on a topic of his choice. Lasting only half an hour, these set pieces were hardly debates as they invariably consisted of a single uninterrupted monologue, answered by the appropriate junior minister in an otherwise empty chamber. London Members were content to linger in the bars or one of the four private dining-rooms where colleagues would be hosting dinners. The more conscientious might catch up with some last-minute research in the Oriel Room, the well-equipped reference library which boasted the most up-to-date information from which to compile a weekend speech, or take the opportunity to borrow a book from the adjoining main library.

None of these were options for Philip North, the Conservative Member for Biddecombe in Devon. Like other government backbenchers he had hurried through the division, called on the second reading of a bill to allow a road bridge to be built across the Humber estuary, in the hope of catching his pair in the Members' Lobby.

The pairing system was as old as party politics, and had been born out of the inconvenience of the way the Commons conducts its business. Divisions at all times of the day and night played havoc with MPs' private lives, if indeed they had one, and pairing had evolved to accommodate

Members who, for whatever reason, were unable to attend a division. Although there had been many demands over the years to reform the ancient, and some would say absurd, method of voting adopted by Members, few changes had been introduced. MPs still had to congregate in one of the two long lobbies beside the chamber itself whenever a division was called, and then wait patiently before moving slowly to the end where clerks took their names, and tellers counted as they passed through a small gap between the lobby doors. One slight relaxation in the procedure of the House had been the extension to eight minutes of the time allowed for Members to reach their respective lobby before the three entrances into each of the two division lobbies were locked shut by one of the Commons' forty-three uniformed doorkeepers. Occasionally ministers who had been forced to abandon some important meeting at a critical moment had demanded a more modern system, perhaps a remote device to register a vote electronically, but none had ever been introduced. The truth was that back-benchers were quite prepared to endure the inconvenience if it meant that ministers suffered too. It also allowed MPs an ideal opportunity to buttonhole elusive members of the government. And North simply felt relieved to have a pair at all.

North waited patiently, scanning the faces for Alun Rees, but he was nowhere to be seen. He checked briefly with the clerk responsible for recording the votes of the L–Z names in the Noe lobby and received confirmation that Rees had been present. 'Damn,' muttered North to himself. Rees must have been quick off the mark tonight, which meant that either the randy old sod had some assignation lined up, or was nursing a pint of best bitter in the Kremlin. North decided to gamble on the latter. Officially known as the Strangers' Bar, the Kremlin was the Labour Party's preferred watering-hole, which left the Tories enjoying a virtual monopoly of the much larger Smoking Room, where visitors were not permitted, and the rather more genteel Pugin Room, appropriated from the House of Lords. North took one last look around the lobby and headed down to the Kremlin.

North arrived to find the Strangers' Bar noisy and filled with smoke. There was only room for a dozen or so to be seated in the two alcoves opposite the bar, and as usual there was a scrum waiting to be served. Almost as soon as he was through the swing door, North spotted Rees at the far end of the bar, trying to make himself heard on the bar telephone. As North elbowed his way through the crowd, apologising briefly to the inebriated Member for one of the Birmingham seats whose drink was spilled as he passed by, Rees replaced the receiver.

'Come to buy me a pint with all your Tory millions?' he asked with uncharacteristic good humour.

North deduced his pair was well lubricated and

had probably been fixing himself a date for the weekend. Although he knew little about Rees's private life, he knew that he was still married, but only just, and that his extracurricular escapades with another Member's secretary had brought him some notoriety a year or so earlier.

'Any time, Alun.' He laughed. 'It'll help salve my conscience before I go back to Devon to grind the faces of the poor.' As he waved to attract the attention of the barman he raised the object of his visit. 'I tried to catch you in the lobby, but I must have just missed you. Are you voting again tonight?'

'If there are any votes tonight, I shan't be there. You can go home, don't worry,' said Rees.

'And what about Monday evening?' pressed North. 'We're on a two line at seven, but I can't get back until ten. Is that okay?'

'Down to Devon to see that pretty wife of yours, eh?' leered Rees. 'You just take your time. I won't vote until you get back. It's only some opposed private business anyway. I don't know why the whips bother.' He picked up the pint jar that North had slid across towards him. 'You can have Wednesday off as well, young man.'

'Got a date?' ventured North. This was as close as he ever reached to inquiring into how Rees spent his time. He wasn't really interested but he felt an obligation not to be unfriendly to his pair . . . the person who was almost as important in North's life as his wife, his offspring . . . and his girlfriend. Once Rees had confided in him, describing the tempestuous relationship with his wife in Wales, and North had wished he hadn't bothered. It was all too tacky, too dreadful. Evidently they existed only in a state of mutual hostility.

'A speaking engagement; North London Polytechnic, actually,' he drawled in his thick, exaggerated Welsh accent. 'Marxists the lot of 'em, but no harm in that, eh?'

'Rather you than me,' murmured North, making his exit and thinking how phoney Rees's accent was. Had he taken elocution lessons, as Harold Wilson had been rumoured to, so as to transform an Oxford don into an acceptable Liverpudlian or, in Rees's case, a lecturer from the Midlands into a bogus boyo from the valleys? He gave Rees a wave goodnight and worked his way back through the crowd to the door. It was to be the last time he saw Alun Rees alive.

Chapter One

The Pair

North left the Commons on Friday morning, safe in the knowledge that there was only private business on the order papers, and there would be no important votes that day. Soon after the division bell had sounded for prayers at nine thirty he had cleared his desk in the cramped cupboard that masqueraded as his office in the Norman Shaw building, some seventy yards from the Commons along the Embankment, and carried his bulging briefcase through the underground tunnels that connected Westminster tube station and pedestrian underpass to the palace itself. Although he had only been in the Commons for two years, North's face was sufficiently well known to the police officer on duty at the top of the steps leading to New Palace Yard that he had no need to extricate his little laminated colour-coded card that identified the holder as a Member. An imposing six-footer with a mane of unruly, ill-brushed hair, North always had a ready smile for the Palace of Westminster's policemen. Each knew every corner of the eight acres that made up their unique beat, and they were an invaluable source of useful intelligence. They knew, often rather sooner than the whips, the exact date that the House would rise for the recess, or the time an adjournment debate would begin. They heard the gossip, and in North's opinion their information was even more reliable than that emanating from the ministerial drivers. There was, therefore, a purpose in North's cheerful 'good morning' as he had stepped into the colonnaded approach to New Palace Yard and sought out the policeman on duty in the box under the canopy of the Members' Entrance. He wanted to know what had happened to Alun Rees.

North had heard the news on Radio 4's *Today* programme. Rees had been killed late the previous evening, too late for the London editions to report it, in what was described as a road accident in Westminster. No further details had been given and instead the BBC's political correspondent had been invited to speculate on the likely date for the by-election, how the new candidates would be selected, and the political consequences for the parties of a mid-term poll in the Cardiff East constituency. MPs cultivated their pairs assiduously, and there was considerable competition among the unpaired to recruit a newly elected Member. Convention dictated that once a Member had found his man on the benches opposite, there could be no poaching. So the death of Rees was likely to constrict North very considerably until the writ had been moved for a by-election, and a successor was elected. Nor was there any guarantee that the replacement would agree to inherit North as a pair. As North pondered gloomily, Rees's successor might be ideologically opposed to pairing or, worse still, one of his own over-eager colleagues might engineer a telephone call to congratulate the newly returned Member on the night of the election, and bag him or her as a pair first. Another favourite scheme was to approach the parliamentary candidate's 'minder', the MP deployed to prowl the constituency throughout the campaign and guide the candidate across the minefield of potential gaffes that invariably accompanied inexperienced politicians seeking a role on the national stage. Grateful candidates learned quickly to take the advice of their minders, whatever the topic, be it sartorial or polemic, and invariably accepted their recommendations for a pair. North would put nothing past some of his more unscrupulous fellow Members.

The death of a Member of Parliament, the *Today* journalist stated, is not an unusual event. The radio pundits calculated that there were usually four by-elections a year, and the statistics over twenty years revealed a steady toll to coronary heart disease, liver failure, cancer and, that more modern scourge, the Provisional IRA. Rees's death had been a little unusual, according to the policeman, in that he had been the victim of a hit-and-run driver while crossing the busy road outside St Stephen's entrance. North had gasped out loud at the news, waking his girlfriend, Debbie Buxton, who was curled up in bed beside him.

'One down and a further two hundred and fifty to go,' she whispered. 'What's the big deal?'

North loved her company, adored her body but never understood why politics bored her. 'Rees was my bloody pair,' muttered North, disconsolate, as he rolled out of bed. 'Life is going to be a lot more awkward without him. He was half cut when I saw him last night. I can guess what happened to the poor old sod.' For whenever an MP died, whatever the public pronouncements about the tragic loss of his unique qualities, his colleagues would only ask two questions. How big was his majority and who was his pair?

'A clever little shit like you can easily get another one, can't you?' she grinned.

'It's not as simple as that,' grumbled North. Not all Opposition Members were willing to pair, and with the government's large majority it meant that a substantial proportion of Members had no one to pair with. For them there was no chance to slip away for a quiet dinner outside Westminster, or to get a decent night's sleep on a Thursday evening when so many MPs, particularly those from Scotland, were anxious to catch the night sleeper. Pairing was no longer an informal arrangement. It had to be approved by the whips and every agreement had to be registered with the whip's clerk.

But he wasn't going to explain the pairing system to Debbie again. He had tried lots of times, but her boredom threshold could not sustain the complexities of the convention. That was partly what made her so attractive to him, apart from her long slim legs, her tiny bottom and pert little breasts. She wasn't interested in politics, and that suited North fine. Nor was she interested in his wife, his family or his other more orthodox life in Devon.

North contemplated the news while he collected his Jaguar from the nearly empty second level of the underground carpark and gave a nonchalant wave of thanks to the policeman who motioned him across the heavy traffic clogging Parliament Square. The officers on duty on the main gate were just as useful as their colleagues indoors. Not only would they clear a way for Members when a division had been called, but they had also been known to use their discretion wisely when certain Members had attempted, unwisely, to drive their cars after dinner. Such incidents never made the newspapers, and the Members were able to recover their car keys the following morning. On this particular bright May morning North calculated that the drive to his constituency would take four hours, subject to the traffic on the elevated section of the M4. He was starting his weekend early, as most MPs did, but there would be little free time. His agent had scheduled a meeting with some planning protesters at four, and then there was the barbecue on Sunday at Biddecombe, as well as his usual constituency business to be done.

His routine was much the same most weekends. A short walk from his flat at the end of Lord North Street, a four-hour sprint down the motorway, and then two days to adjust to Devon's pace before returning to London on Monday morning in time to attend Questions in the afternoon. The drive was uneventful, apart from the usual crop of disappointed caravan owners standing forlornly beside their overheating cars on the hard shoulder of the M5, and North found his thoughts drifting to Rees's death.

The policeman on duty at the Members' Entrance had told him that particular stretch, by St Stephen's entrance, was notorious for accidents, although the victims were usually unwary tourists straying into the bus lane, or over-confident dispatch riders picked off by aggressive mini-cabs. There was no pavement beside the road, and the only physical protection available was limited to a few steel crush-barriers designed to herd visitors waiting for gallery tickets into an orderly queue. There had been calls for traffic lights to be installed but whatever action was taken now would come too late for poor old Rees.

He had been knocked down just after eleven when, North presumed, he had been returning to his office in Great College Street, some two hundred yards from the Lords. Several colleagues had only narrowly escaped a similar fate, and the infamous quarter-mile was sometimes known as by-election alley.

North recalled how he had first met the red-haired Welshman, while they were both trying to while away the hours on an RAF VC-10 between Ascension and the Falklands. The Ministry of Defence often arranged flights for MPs so they could be shown how well the tax-payers' money was being spent at the huge military encampment outside Port Stanley. As on most delegations, the political parties had been represented equally, thus ensuring that the voting figures in the divisions were unaffected by the absentees. This was another, more institutionalised version of pairing, and one that was worked out by the so-called 'usual channels' of Opposition and government whips operating behind the scenes.

While the excursion was a pleasant enough diversion from Westminster, and one that was sanctioned by the whips, it involved hour upon hour in the air, facing backwards and without alcohol. North had only learned that the RAF was 'dry' at Brize Norton, when it had been too late to do anything about it, but Rees had come well prepared. He had brought a flask of what he claimed was ice-cold ginger ale and a pocket chess set. Once aboard, North had found himself seated next to Rees, and they had played chess and shared the whisky together. While the RAF crew and the ministry minder had almost certainly suspected the subterfuge, no one had dared challenge Rees.

North admitted to himself that it would have been an exaggeration to suggest that he had ever really liked Rees. He had been a convenient, occasional drinking companion and he was an able chess player, but they had never played against each other again. Politics apart, they had little else in common and although North had not bothered to check Rees's age in *Dodd's, Who's Who* or any of the other standard works of reference, he judged that he must be nearly ten years older than himself, which put him in his late forties. Age mattered little in the Commons, unless someone was eyeing the title and privileges of the Father of the House; Members judged their colleagues by political reliability, behaviour and, that most intangible of qualities, clubbiness.

Rees had fared well, in North's estimation. He had been consistent, that most important of virtues. Professional politicians hate being surprised, and no matter how extreme, no matter how eccentric, it's crucial that Members should conform to type. Rebels should rebel, bores should be boring, the eloquent should never disappoint and the pompous should lose none of their pomp.

For a militant suddenly to adopt moderation, or a centrist to endorse extremism was too disconcerting. The whips liked their Members to fit into neat categories, and so did the rest of the House if it would but admit it, thought North.

Although quite young by the Labour Party's standards, Rees had fixed himself firmly in the middle ground. He had been a lecturer at a technical college in Sunderland before being adopted as a candidate in Cardiff, and had allied himself to the soft left in the Parliamentary Labour Party. He had willingly accepted North's pairing proposal, made on the return leg from the Falklands while refuelling at Wideawake. Rees had later admitted that although he had been warned against pairing by some of the more hardline of his intake, he had decided to because he usually shared a car to Wales with two other neighbouring MPs, and they liked to set off home after the last division on Thursday night. North suspected that Rees might have had another motive. He had heard a rumour that some MPs used a car pool but claimed individual travel expenses, an exercise that enabled those with constituencies some distance from London to pocket a tidy sum tax-free every week.

North admonished himself for thinking ill of Rees, and tried instead to recall his parliamentary performance. It had been lacklustre, but he had been steadfast in his opposition to the wave of nationalist violence that had swept Wales in recent months. The Welsh-language extremists had been his target, and Rees had been unambiguous in his condemnation of the campaign of arson that had wrecked so many remote Welsh cottages. Some Tories believed their political opponents were soft on some forms of terrorism, but Rees had gained the respect of the House when he had made a withering attack on the fanatics during one of the broadcasted debates. Was it a second reading? North couldn't recall. He hadn't been in the chamber at the time, but he had heard colleagues mention the speech later. North was slightly ashamed that he had not taken the trouble to obtain a copy of the relevant *Hansard* afterwards, and congratulate his pair. It was all part of the Westminster etiquette to give encouragement to those who had made even the most mediocre contribution to a debate. Affability outside the chamber, whatever the atmosphere inside, was the key to good relations with one's political enemies, wherever they lurked. Some saw no need to be polite, while others thought it demeaning or hypocritical, but North genuinely enjoyed the company of those with whom he had little, in political terms, in common. There was also an element of expediency in this. North reminded himself that he would have to brush up on his parliamentary manners if he was to catch another pair.

Rees, he knew, had a wife in Cardiff, and two small children, but that was about it apart from usual parliamentary gossip about who was sleeping with whom. Nor was that surprising. There were not many authentic cross-party friendships in the modern Commons. Their backgrounds, for a start, had been worlds apart. The son of a regular soldier, North had been to Ampleforth, the Catholic public school in Yorkshire, and had been taught by Benedictine monks; Rees had been to a secondary modern in Coventry and had worked as an apprentice in the British Rail engineering depot where his father had been a foreman. North had obtained a poor second in PPE at London before joining the BBC as a production assistant in the General Features Department, starting his broadcasting career with a popular science programme on BBC1. Rees had gone to teacher-training college, spent a year at Ruskin College, Oxford, and had been sponsored by a left-orientated charity to research and write a paper about housing policy. He had been adopted as a parliamentary candidate because of an internal struggle between two factions on the General Management Committee which had divided the local party and created an opening for a compromise figure not obviously from either side. His Welsh ancestry had helped, as had his commitment to move back to Wales once he had been elected.

For North the path to his safe seat in Devon had been more fortuitous. He had a novelty value for most local Conservative associations because few believed there were really any Tories in the BBC. He had once told his wife, half seriously, that he suspected he had been invited to several party functions just to satisfy the inquisitiveness of a local committee member who had spotted him on television. Having harnessed his public-speaking skills, he had become a minor hit on the after-dinner speaking circuit. That had led to the mandatory unsuccessful shot at the hopelessly unwinnable seat of Dunfermline, and permission from Central Office to apply for interviews to more attractive constituencies. The retirement of old Sir Reggie Aird at the last election had given North that most coveted of political attributes, a handsome majority. That, and an appreciation of Tom Sharpe's caustic wit, was about all North had shared with Rees.

On some Fridays the press would call North on his car telephone for a comment on a current story, but on this particular day his journey was undisturbed. The Sundays' lobby correspondents were no doubt busy preparing themselves for the usual Friday afternoon off-the-record briefing from the Prime Minister's Press Secretary, and little had happened in the chamber during the week to excite the West Country hacks. So, even though North was known to be a captive in his car for the duration of his regular Friday trip down the motorway, he received just one call. His constituency agent rang from his office in the market town of Netherton to confirm his ETA.

Agents were like that. They invariably distrusted their Member's ability to read his own diary, or be punctual for meetings that had been arranged months in advance. But George Singleton need not have worried. His member, Phil North, was rather more reliable than most.

North arrived in Netherton in plenty of time, and listened patiently while the group of protesters outlined their grievance: a site at the edge of the town had been acquired by a developer and he had made a planning application to build twenty-two houses. The residents were furious but, like every case of its kind, there were those who were keen to let the building work go ahead. The local shop was enthusiastic about the prospect of more custom and the farmer who owned the field stood to make a killing. North was sympathetic to the protesters, and gently pointed out that this was strictly a matter for Netherton's district council and its planning committee. He enjoyed a good relationship with his councillors, but that would not survive if he interfered with what was purposely a local decision-making process and took sides in a contentious planning dispute. But the conversation that was to upset North, and preoccupy him for most of Sunday night and his return drive to London, would occur at Biddecombe on Sunday evening.

Unlike so many constituency events taking place up and down the country, where the Member of

Parliament dutifully paraded his wife before their political supporters, said a few appropriate words of encouragement before distributing the raffle prizes and tried to balance a glass of warm white wine while struggling with a burnt sausage, those held in south Devon were distinguished by the large number of up-country visitors they attracted. Whether a wine and cheese party or a coffee morning, it was never a case of the same old faces. So many of his constituents were retired, and had grown-up children, and probably grandchildren too, that weekend functions were not the struggle against boredom that made them unpopular with MPs' wives in so many places. North could always anticipate meeting several new interesting people. And the Sunday barbecue was no different. After murmuring a few pleasantries to the branch chairman he was introduced to a rather younger man, perhaps in his late twenties, who had been brought to the party by his mother, whom he was visiting for a few days. James Watson, so he told him, worked for the Forensic Science Service as a technical assistant in the Lambeth Road laboratory in south-east London.

Usually North avoided socialising with civil servants. They rarely had any good news and there was often an awkward moment when some indiscretion was imparted, leaving North wondering whether he had just received a calculated leak, or merely had been embarrassed by a too-garrulous minion. But James Watson was not the run-of-the-mill civil servant who seized any opportunity to complain to politicians about how underfunded their particular branch was, or how misunderstood they were. Instead he opened with a trite remark about the world being so small, leaving North to ponder for a moment what the connection was between the two that they shared. Had Watson appeared on North's programme while he had been working at the BBC? Or had the link been in a parliamentary context? North looked deliberately quizzical, and prompted Watson to explain that they had met briefly at the Lime Grove studios when he had presented a television documentary on the work of the Home Office's most anonymous department. That particular programme had been screened some three years ago, North remembered, and he had not the slightest recollection of Watson, although he tactfully feigned otherwise, a skill at which he, like most politicians, was necessarily adept.

But Watson had pressed the matter further. That was not their only connection. Why, only the previous afternoon he had completed the toxicological screening on Alun Rees. As well as being slightly taken aback at Watson's disclosure, North was also intrigued.

'Does the Home Office always screen the victims of hit-and-run drivers?' he asked.

The first part of Watson's reply explained their policy. 'Any unnatural death is routinely the subject of a coroner's inquest in England and Wales, and that means an alcohol and drug screen conducted in one of our labs, either in Chepstow or the Lambeth Road. In certain cases, like that of the late Alun Rees, a more comprehensive test for toxic substances was made.'

'Why Rees?' queried North.

'He'd been drinking, and his blood-alcohol level was more than double the legal limit of thirty-five micrograms for driving. But he had also been taking drugs.'

That revelation had been the bombshell that had left North stunned. 'Are you sure? I saw him less than an hour before his death, and although he was pretty tight he certainly wasn't high on drugs.'

'What we found in him wouldn't make him high. It killed him,' said the technician. 'The late Alun Rees was poisoned, and that's exactly what we reported to the police last night.'

Instead of driving back up to London late on Monday morning in order to miss the rush-hour congestion around Bristol and Reading, as was his practice, North kissed his wife and nine-year-old daughter goodbye soon after dawn and headed up the motorway early. Neither had complained, for they both accepted that an MP's life was not his own. Cassandra, who was a partner in a firm of solicitors in Exeter, knew better than to try and interfere with his diary while the House was sitting and if she knew about her husband's affair with Deborah she gave no hint of it.

North's London flat was in a mansion block overlooking Smith Square, conveniently close to the Commons and equipped with a division bell that allowed him to get across to the chamber in the designated eight minutes when a vote had been called. It was sparsely decorated, as he had been determined not to allow his life to become dominated by Westminster. If the flat was slightly uncomfortable, so Cass had reasoned, there would be a greater incentive to go down to Devon each weekend, even though North needed no encouragement to abandon London at the weekend. Their cottage in Prince's Tor, just outside Netherton, was quite ideal, and close enough to the railway station at Newton Abbot for Cass to commute to her office in Exeter, leaving Francesca in the hands of the Polish student who was their temporary au pair.

Sensitive of the need to be careful about his personal security, North left his car in the huge five-level carpark under New Palace Yard and strolled home to prepare all the mail that had accumulated in Devon for dictation the following morning. He then spent a solitary evening in front of the television, rose early the next morning and walked along the Embankment to Norman Shaw, the building that had once housed New Scotland Yard and now provided office accommodation for some two hundred Members and their staff. North had a ground-floor room with a view over the inner courtyard, with its permanently closed wrought-iron gates and, in the other direction, he could just see the entrance to what had been Cannon Row police station. Now it was a gym for unfit MPs. Ten years earlier North had come to know that particular building quite well. When he had joined the Metropolitan Police as a Special Constable he had undergone his training there, two evenings a week for six gruelling months.

It was to the police that North made his first telephone call. He dialled New Scotland Yard, and asked for Detective Chief Superintendent Thompson. A moment later he was being connected to him.

'Good morning, Chief Superintendent. My name is Philip North. You may not recall but we met quite some time ago when I worked for the BBC and made a programme about genetic fingerprinting.'

'I remember you well, Mr North,' replied the policeman courteously. All policemen were always exercising caution when dealing with politicians. 'And now you're the Member for, er, South Devon, isn't it? How can I help you?'

'Biddecombe,' corrected North. 'It's a long time since my service with the Specials and I wondered if you can advise me on who is the officer in charge of a particular inquiry.'

'I'll do my best. What's the investigation?' His

voice reflected a distinct change in tone. Being asked for information by an MP was not likely to be career-threatening.

'The murder of Alun Rees,' said North shortly. What delicate way was there to discuss such a subject? he mused.

'Murder, is it?' said Thompson, now back on his guard. 'I thought there had been a traffic accident, if we're talking about the MP who was killed last Thursday.'

'I've been told it's more complicated, and I need to speak to whoever's conducting the inquiry.'

'Well, I doubt it's the Yard unless this was a political assassination, in which case it'll be the lads upstairs from Special Branch. But under normal circumstances a murder would be handled by the local CID. If I remember correctly he was run down outside the Commons, wasn't he?'

'That's right. Hit and run, as they say.'

'Then that will be A District, and Rochester Row most likely. The public doesn't realise it, but the Yard is only the Commissioner's Office. It's not even a police station. I'll find out if it is Rochester Row and call you back. It may take a few minutes.' Thompson needed to take advice on this. Dealing with politicians required all the skills of careful handling more usually found in the Bomb Squad and murder was a sensitive issue under any circumstances, so he would need to log a call such as this and mention it to another senior officer . . . just in case.

'I'd be very grateful, Superintendent. You're very kind.'

'No problem. I'll phone you as soon as I have found out. Can I get you at the Commons?'

Ten minutes later Thompson called back with the information North had requested. 'You're quite right, the Rees case is being handled as a murder inquiry, although that news has not been released yet. Detective Chief Inspector Young is in charge and I think he would like to see you. Can you give him a call now at Rochester Row? His direct line is 230 4782.'

'Do you know why he wants to speak to me?' asked North innocently.

'At a guess I'd say it's because you knew this death was a murder – when not even the family had been told, let alone the press. I expect he'll want to know how you found out, but that's for him to ask you.'

'Let's hope that hasn't made me a suspect,' replied North, ending the conversation on a casual note. The trouble was, it suddenly dawned on him that his call had probably done just that.

Chapter Two

The Speaker

As North left the chamber, soon after the conclusion of Education Questions, he rang DCI Young from one of the telephones in the Members' Lobby. They agreed to meet that same afternoon in one of the small interview rooms in Norman Shaw set aside for Members to talk to their constituents with a degree of privacy that was not possible in their shared offices. North's room-mate was Toby Bellington, an older Member on his third parliament, and Jim Knox, an ambitious young barrister who had already been appointed Parliamentary Private Secretary to a junior minister in the Department of Employment. Although all three were rarely in the room at the same time, it would have been quite impossible to see the CID man with the possibility of one of them barging in at any moment, especially if this murder was to be kept quiet.

North had a meeting of an All-Party Group to attend in Westminster Hall, but he slipped away early, with a nod of apology to the chairman and a glance at the annunciator in the corner, the implication being that he was hoping to speak in the debate on the economy that had got under way. Instead he hastened back to his office to be told by the attendant on duty at the door that he had two visitors in the interview room. As he entered, Detective Chief Inspector Young rose to his feet and introduced himself to North.

'Good afternoon, sir. This is Detective Inspector Shawcross who is assisting my investigation.' He motioned to a younger man, also in a shiny suit and one of those special ties policemen award themselves after particularly interesting cases. Young's emblem, what looked like a cosh over some laurels, told those in the know that he had been part of the team that had searched for Lord Lucan. Young got straight to the point. 'I wonder if you could tell me how well you knew Alun Rees?'

'Hardly at all, Chief Inspector,' replied North. 'He was my pair, but we rarely socialised. He was active on environmental issues, and he had worked to help protect the dolphins off the Welsh coast. Apart from that, I can't say he was a particularly well-known parliamentarian or a contributor to debates, except on Welsh affairs. Probably a good constituency man . . . I couldn't honestly say. But certainly not one of the loony left. You would be better off talking to one of his colleagues on the Opposition benches.'

'I shall be,' confirmed the detective. 'But first, could you tell me how you came to contact Detective Superintendent Thompson this morning?'

'I wanted to talk to you, that's why,' responded North. 'I had been told that Alun Rees had been murdered, not run down in an accident, and I wanted to have a word. I think I might have some information that is relevant.'

'Go on, sir,' prompted Young. 'But perhaps you could start by telling me when you last saw him.'

'I saw him on the night he died. He was in the Strangers' Bar and I bought him a drink. He was already quite plastered, but that wasn't what I wanted to tell you.'

'There was something else?' queried the detective.

'Yes. Two years ago we both went to the Falklands together on a sort of inspection tour, to see the troops. Most MPs are offered the chance at some stage. While we were there we were entertained royally in the officers' mess of one of the battalions stationed down there. We had had a long day and Rees was quite a heavy drinker.'

Young nodded. 'We know.'

'Well, on this occasion I had to help him get to bed. We were both sharing a room in the accommodation block, and he was a trifle indiscreet.' North hesitated.

'And this is relevant to our inquiries?' Young's voice was smooth, encouraging.

'It may be. I can't be sure. He told me that he and his wife didn't get along. In fact he said he hated her.'

'Yes, and . . .'

'Well, I don't really suppose he meant it, but he said that he'd have to kill her before she killed him. Looking back on it, I'm sure this was just the liquor talking. He never mentioned it again and I rather assumed that he had been speaking in jest.'

'Really, sir?' mused Young. 'Did you report this conversation at the time?'

'Report it? Who to? The man was drunk as a skunk and could hardly stand up. He hadn't actually threatened anyone, after all. It was just that he loathed his wife and the feeling was mutual. That's not an uncommon condition, Chief Inspector.'

'True,' the police officer murmured. 'I occasionally think the worst of mine, but that's another matter. I was really trying to establish that there is no actual record of this conversation you had with Rees.'

'Certainly not. He obviously had no idea of what he had said the next morning. We never spoke of it again.'

'Very well, sir. Thank you for your co-operation. There is one other matter. Can you tell me how you learned that Mr Rees had been murdered?'

This was not a question that North had been looking forward to. 'I was told, in confidence, by a civil servant. Someone who had access to the pathology tests.'

'A leak, in other words,' said Young scornfully.

'And just for the record, where were you when Rees died?'

'He was killed on Thursday night, wasn't he? Last week.'

'Yes. We have the time of death as ten past eleven.'

'Well, I voted in the ten o'clock division, and then I went down to the Kremlin to find Alun.'

'The Kremlin, sir?'

'Oh, I'm sorry. It's the Strangers' Bar. There are nineteen bars and restaurants in the Palace of Westminster and this particular one is known as the Kremlin. We all call it that.'

'Might one ask why?' inquired Young.

'It's because it's a favourite haunt of the Labour Party. It serves draught bitter and it's got a rather more congenial atmosphere than the Smoking Room upstairs. There was a possibility of another division at about eleven, before the adjournment debate, and we were on two lines so I couldn't go home.'

'Two lines?'

'Our whipping. We get sent the business for the House each week, and the number of underlines indicates its importance. One line means the government can cope without you. Two means you can be absent if you're paired, and three lines promises a difficult interview with the Chief Whip if you fail to turn up.'

'But if Rees was your pair,' interrupted Shaw-cross, 'why weren't you paired with him?'

'I intended to see him at the ten o'clock division to find out what his voting intentions were later in the evening. I must have just missed him so I went to the Kremlin to find him and come to an arrangement. We are,' North corrected himself, 'sorry, were, very informal. We'd always vote at ten, and then probably see what the score was for sitting late. Sometimes we get an early night, and we can go straight after the division. More likely, with the pressure of legislation from this government, we would have been kept quite late. In any event, just because we're on two lines, Rees might have been on three.'

'What effect would that have had?'

'It means he wouldn't have been free to pair. The system only works when both sides are on one- or two-line whips.'

'This is all beyond me,' Young muttered. 'I need to know whether he had any enemies. Apart from Mrs Rees, have you any ideas? Any nutters about?'

'Surely you don't think someone around here poisoned him?'

'Poison?' said Young sharply. 'Who said anything about poison?'

'My source mentioned that Rees had been poisoned. A potent toxin had been found during the post-mortem.'

Young exchanged glances with his detective inspector. 'Your source was not entirely correct. It's true that Rees was found to have a large quantity of thallium in his organs, and although that would have killed him eventually, it was not actually the cause of death. He died because pressure had been applied to the carotid artery.'

'You mean Rees wasn't run down, or poisoned . . . he was strangled?'

'Not quite strangled. Just enough force on that pressure point.' Young placed a finger on the side of his neck, close to his ear. 'It blocks the flow of blood to the head and death follows quite quickly. Rees was already unconscious because of being hit by the car, but according to our forensic evidence, he was still alive after the impact.'

'So you're really looking for three murderers: the person who ran him down, whoever administered the thallium, and someone who was on the scene straight after the crash.'

'It's actually rather more complicated than that,' said Young thoughtfully. 'We recovered Mr Rees's car from the Members' carpark on Saturday. It had been fitted with a bomb. It would seem that either Mr Rees had a great many enemies, or he was the victim of a very determined killer.'

'My God, what an incredible situation. Have you any leads yet?'

'Provided you are willing to keep this conversation confidential, Mr North, I can tell you that we have a sight too many clues. Although the hit-and-run driver was not seen by any of the witnesses, we do know that the car was probably a Mercedes, and we have part of its registration number. I'm quite confident we'll trace the vehicle. But immediately after the accident several people went to Mr Rees's aid. A policeman was one of the first there, and he was emphatic that Rees was still alive. He checked his pulse, saw that Rees was losing consciousness, and returned to his box at the entrance to the Lords carpark where he telephoned for an ambulance. That took a few moments, and by the time he had returned a small crowd had gathered and Rees was dead. He took the names and addresses of some of those at the scene, but he thinks several spectators drifted away as he made his notes.'

'So in your view the murderer happened to be conveniently close to Rees when he was struck by the Mercedes.'

Young hesitated before replying. 'There are several possibilities. The murderer might have been stalking Rees, and then seized the opportunity when it presented itself; or he might have been working in league with a partner driving the car. Either way there is a possibility that the murderer had some medical knowledge. Finding the carotid artery is difficult for the uninitiated.'

'You realise, Chief Inspector, that there are considerable implications to your first hypothesis, that the murderer was following Rees?'

'Explain,' demanded Young.

'Rees came out of St Stephen's entrance, which is the main public entrance for the Central Lobby. But unless the murderer was waiting outside in the road, it suggests either that the murderer was someone who could follow Rees out of the Members' Lobby, or he was waiting for Rees in the Central Lobby or St Stephen's Hall.'

'I don't see the difference,' said Young, looking puzzled. 'You're going to have to explain where the public can and can't go in the Commons.'

'Suppose you reconstruct Rees's route from the moment he had voted in the ten o'clock division, to where he was killed. He would have walked from the chamber straight into the Members' Lobby. Then to the Kremlin Bar and back to the lobby. The only people allowed there are Members, former Members and lobby correspondents. But the journalists are kept in the library corridor during the actual division, and are not allowed to cross the lobby.'

'Which implies that the only person who could follow Rees out of the Members' Lobby would have to be another Member of Parliament . . . or a former Member?'

'Exactly. Former Members are entitled to access to the Members' Lobby, but I doubt there would be a record of whether one was visiting last week. As for sitting MPs, that gives you six hundred and forty-eight possible suspects.'

'As many as that?' said Young in surprise.

'I'm excluding the Speaker,' replied North. 'He couldn't be arrested even if he'd committed the crime.'

The DCI overlooked the remark. 'Anybody else

allowed into the Members' Lobby?'

'Only visitors to one of the special galleries. Most of the public galleries are reached through the Central Lobby, but there are a few seats reserved for special visitors, usually overseas delegations or a Member's special guest. They are escorted across the Members' Lobby, but they're not allowed in while there is a division in progress.'

'And then Rees would have walked from the Members' Lobby to the Central Lobby?'

'Yes. That's where Members meet their constituents and the public. Anyone can go there, but there is an attendant on duty to take the names of those seeking an appointment, and there are plenty of police on duty supervising the crowds.'

'So someone could wait in the Central Lobby and get a clear view of Members walking to and from the division?'

'They would have a better view during the division. The big double swing doors between the Members' Lobby and the Central Lobby are let open once a division has been called. Anyone waiting in the Central Lobby could sit on one of the benches there and wait for Rees to emerge. They could also wait in St Stephen's Hall.'

'Where's that?'

'It's a long gallery that connects St Stephen's entrance to the Central Lobby. It's built on the site of the old St Stephen's Chapel which was the first permanent home of the House of Commons. Now it's lined with visitors waiting for a seat in the public gallery.'

'Could Rees have used any other route to get to St Stephen's entrance?'

'Several. The Palace of Westminster is a labyrinth . . . a thousand rooms and two miles of corridors, but if we assume that Rees was taking the shortest route to his office, which was in Great College Street, he would have had to go through the Central Lobby. He would also have had to if he went the rather longer way through the Lords.'

'Why would he have used that?'

'It's covered, that's all. If it was really bucketing down—'

'And it wasn't,' interrupted Young.

'—Members are allowed to go through the Lords and emerge at the Norman Porch under the Victoria Tower, which is slightly closer to Great College Street. You still have to get wet, but there's about fifty yards in it.'

'So if Rees was followed into the street, it could have been by a member of the public from the Central Lobby or St Stephen's Hall, or an MP from the Members' Lobby.'

'That's true, but there is a small catch here. How could the murderer be sure that Rees would go through the Central Lobby? There are three other main exits out of the Members' Lobby, so unless the murderer was sure Rees would be going back to his office, there was only a slim chance that he would be spotted. Someone could wait all day in St Stephen's Hall or the Central Lobby without seeing their Member.'

'Which implies either that the killer was willing to wait a long time in the Central Lobby or the hall on the off-chance of meeting Rees, which would have been dangerous for him, or that this was simply an opportunistic nutter.'

'We have plenty of nutcases to deal with,' said North. 'Our job attracts them. Usually they're quite harmless, and the technical term for them is paraphrenic. They're rational on almost all subjects except for one, when they lose touch with reality.'

'Sounds like a few politicians I've come across,' murmured Young.

North ignored the remark. 'They're easy to spot once you know about them. They all display the same unreasonable behaviour, and write to the Prime Minister and the Queen. Quite often there is an ancient legal dispute at the heart of the problem, and everyone has conspired to deny the paraphrenic justice. On all other topics they appear perfectly normal, and every MP has his share of them.'

'So there are plenty of paraphrenics hanging around the Central Lobby?' asked the detective.

'You would have to talk to your uniformed colleagues on duty there, but my guess is that there are always two or three in attendance. They're usually quite harmless.' North knew of several himself, but they were only excluded if they became rowdy. Most were very dignified, and determined to exercise their democratic right to lobby their MP. Fortunately for those MPs like North blessed with constituencies well away from London, the hazard of 'loops in the lobby' was minimal.

'Perhaps this one wasn't,' said Young, turning to Shawcross. 'Can you make a note of this. We'll need to trace everyone who went into the public gallery last Thursday evening. And the special galleries. And we'll need the names of everyone in the Central Lobby around ten o'clock.'

'Surely you don't think Rees was the victim of a random killer?' asked North with disbelief.

'Oh, no,' corrected Young. 'There's no question of that. The poison wasn't administered opportunistically and putting the pressure on the carotid artery needed technical knowledge. I've seen a photograph of the bruise it left. There's no doubt that we are dealing with a very calculating killer here. As for the bomb, I'm not so sure.'

'Could that have been the IRA?' suggested the MP.

'Frankly I doubt it.' Young wondered how much more he should disclose to the man. 'Rees was not on their hit list, according to Special Branch, although the composition of the bomb is classic Provisional tradecraft: Semtex in a plastic lunchbox fitted with a mercury-switched detonator. Simple but lethal.'

'Does anyone else use Semtex?' asked North, fascinated. It was not often he had the opportunity to learn about the police's forensic skills.

'Virtually every terrorist group in Europe,' conceded the detective ruefully. 'It's made in Czechoslovakia and is very distinctive. Its chemical constituents are patented so we can identify it very quickly, but it's more difficult to trace the bomb-makers themselves. Apart from the Provisionals, who are the most obvious suspects, there are the Sons of Glendower.'

'The Welsh Nationalist extremists?' North had heard of them vaguely, from way back.

'They have a history of bomb-making,' said Young, 'and I understand from the Branch that Rees was very outspoken about their activities. A by-election in Wales would be an opportunity to gain widespread media coverage of their campaign, so the Sons of Glendower have to be in the frame.'

'And if it wasn't political?' added North.

'Statistically, most murders are domestic. A husband, lover or girlfriend. Random killing is not a white, Anglo-Saxon phenomenon. The figures for our clear-up rate in England are really very impressive. The victim will almost certainly have known his or her assailant, and will probably have been a lover or equally likely a member of the immediate family. We don't usually have too far to look. A forensic scientist can examine the body and the scene and give us a remarkably accurate profile of the killer.'

'So profiling is now respectable?' North recalled that initially there had been some opposition to the practice when it was first introduced in English forces.

'New forensic techniques are only adopted after they have been tried and tested. And there's no arguing with profiling. It certainly worked for a murder inquiry I led last year. The experts were meticulous and told me the culprit was likely to be a short, white male, aged twenty-five to thirty-five, right-handed and with a dysfunctional family background. He was an unmarried loner of above-average intelligence but with a fairly menial job such as a car mechanic and possibly prone to mildly obsessive behaviour patterns. We knew his blood type and when we identified a short list of suspects, a DNA test eliminated the innocent parties. The profile was accurate in virtually every respect.'

'But the forensic experts can't help in this case,' concluded North.

'In terrorist cases the forensic people can accumulate the microscopic evidence needed to bring charges and obtain a conviction, but most terrorists are motivated by something other than a defective personality, or so we are told.'

'So you can profile a poisoner or a strangler, but not a bomber?'

'Broadly,' agreed Young, with some reluctance. 'Political motives are rather hard to fathom.'

North was conscious of the ambiguity of the reply. 'So this case is quite a challenge,' he said neutrally.

'At this stage it certainly seems to be,' the detective replied cautiously. 'And the circumstances are quite unique in my experience. Which leads me to a request.'

'Go ahead,' offered the MP.

'I wonder if I might ask you to make a few discreet inquiries on my behalf, among your colleagues. There are too many Commons procedures here for my liking. Who is allowed where, and when. There's so much we need to know but there simply isn't time. I've already had a warning that this incident is under the jurisdiction of the Speaker and not the Commissioner. Would you be willing to help?'

'I'd be pleased to, Chief Inspector. I was once in the Specials, you know. What was then B Division.'

Young sniffed dismissively. 'Did you see much CID work there? I thought the Specials in Chelsea patrolled the King's Road for dates.'

North was ready for the detective's attitude towards the volunteers. Not all the regulars held the part-timers in high regard. Some even referred to them contemptuously as 'hobby-bobbies'. 'As a matter of fact I did. There was a case in Swan Court once that I handled. I was the first on the scene at what was supposed to be a suicide, and I spotted that in fact there had been a murder. The DS on duty that evening was quite prepared to accept the whole scene as it was meant to appear, but I talked him round and he got a conviction.'

Young looked mildly impressed. 'What happened?'

'I had been called to the block of flats by the caretaker who was suspicious that the occupant's curtains hadn't been drawn all day. I broke in and found a man sitting on a sofa with a shotgun between his legs, and most of his neck missing. When the police surgeon arrived he declared the case to be one of suicide, and that was going to be that. But I went through the dead man's desk, while waiting for the coroner's mortuary men to arrive, and I realised from his letters that he had been gay.'

'Gays have a tendency to desperation and suicide in my experience,' remarked Young unsympathetically.

'Indeed,' replied North. 'But this was murder. I noticed that although both barrels of the over-and-under shotgun were dirty, there had only been one cartridge in the breech. I checked further, and I could see that both firing pins were extended, and had been used. Someone had shot the man twice, and then removed the second cartridge to make it look as though there had been a single gunshot.'

'On the basis that suicides usually only pull the trigger once.'

'Having persuaded the DS, he then traced the boyfriend, who promptly confessed, and was subsequently convicted.'

'Very well.' The detective smiled. 'You've convinced me. You're a sleuth at heart. What I need from you is an accurate reconstruction of where Rees was likely to have been during the week before his death. I need his appointments, dinner engagements, voting record, the lot. We need to know his whereabouts in detail right up to ten past eleven Thursday night.'

'Very well. I'll do my best,' replied the MP.

'But before you do that, I'd like your help on a related matter. I had a note from the Assistant Commissioner Crime this morning asking me to liaise with Mr Speaker. As I mentioned it seems that this incident is strictly his jurisdiction.'

'Of course,' explained North, who recognised this was Young's way of seeking help. 'Technically the Commons is part of a royal palace, so the Palace of Westminster has rather a strange extra-legal status. It is one of the unique quirks of history that nobody dies within its precincts. On the very rare occasion that someone does expire within the building, the official record always shows that they left the precincts alive, and actually died elsewhere, usually in hospital. It's one of those old traditions that are the bedrock of Parliament, like the one which prevents Members from referring to the monarch in their speeches. This may seem anachronistic to you,' apologised North, 'but that's the way it is. Mr Speaker's first duty is to protect the rights and privileges of a sovereign parliament.'

The two detectives exchanged glances. 'We're here to identify a killer and bring him to justice. That we will have to answer to the Speaker instead of the Commissioner is academic to us. It's still the same job. Perhaps you would be kind enough to explain what has happened to the Speaker. We have more important things to do right now than worry about ritual and protocol. For a start we're due to interview Mrs Rees in an hour.'

'In Cardiff?' said North with surprise.

'She's in London, staying with her parents. They live in Wandsworth.'

'May I come?' asked North.

Young and Shawcross seemed to have anticipated the request. It would be irregular, but there was no reason why an MP's widow shouldn't have one of her late husband's colleagues present when the police gave their condolences. 'If you can fix the Speaker, I'll pick you up at five fifteen.'

'You have a deal, Chief Inspector,' grinned North.

Having escorted the two policemen to the entrance of Norman Shaw, North wasted no time in ringing the doorkeeper at the Back of the Chair to check who was on duty. He established that Mr Deputy Speaker had taken over half an hour ago, and put a call through to the Speaker's secretary and arranged to see him urgently. Five minutes later he had emerged from the pedestrian tunnel into New Palace Yard, and was striding towards the ornate doorway to Speaker's House, the epicentre of power in the mother of parliaments. As he reached the top of the red-carpeted staircase the Speaker's Trainbearer, who was waiting at the top, ushered him into the antique lift and led him down a passage lined with portraits of maharajahs and Indian potentates to a small study. After a few moments, Mr Speaker appeared through a side door, dressed in his frock coat, britches and silk ruffles at his neck.

Although perhaps a slightly comical figure to the television viewer, the Speaker wielded true power. It was he alone who decided who would, and would not, be called in debates and during Questions. Each morning at eleven he convened a meeting attended by his secretary, the two Deputy Speakers, the three clerks and their deputies, to discuss the day's business, but it was the Speaker who exercised the final say on the composition of the list of those to be called to speak. A backbencher could only expect to catch his eye perhaps twice a year at Prime Minister's Questions, so the displeasure of the Speaker could be manifested in a period of imposed silence. Nor was there any appeal to a higher authority. There was none in this matter, beyond the will of the House as expressed in a division. And on the rare occasion a division was called to challenge Mr Speaker's ruling, the House was expected to support him. Any other result but an overwhelming vote of confidence in him would lead to his resignation and a minor constitutional crisis. North visibly shuddered at the prospect of defying the Speaker. And, he reminded himself, this Mr Speaker was likely to be around for some time, his re-election and reappointment after the next general election being a mere formality. North knew that of all the uncertainties in British parliamentary life, there was one absolute: it would not be worth crossing him.

'I do hope this is urgent, Philip,' he said pleasantly. 'I'm entertaining the Speaker of Bermuda's House of Assembly to tea. This is really not a very good moment.'

'I'm so sorry, Mr Speaker,' he replied formally, 'but it is urgent. As you know, Alun Rees was murdered—'

'That's supposed to be a secret,' said Mr Speaker grimly. He stroked his silver hair slowly, a sure sign in the chamber that the Speaker was on edge. It was one that was ignored at the peril of the minister or backbencher.

'Of course, as secrets go in this place it hasn't got a very long shelf life. The press gallery will have it soon,' said the younger man with the appropriate mixture of deference and flippancy. He knew the Speaker enjoyed his company.

Mr Speaker muttered something under his

breath about journalists that North couldn't catch, and shook his head. 'This is all very bad for the House, you know. There hasn't been a murder here since 1812, when the Prime Minister was shot in the lobby. It's not good at all.'

North nodded sympathetically. 'I've been asked by the police to help them.'

'Not "help them with their inquiries" I hope,' he said with a trace of uncharacteristic sarcasm. 'The chap who was hanged for shooting Spencer Perceval was a bankrupt madman. I hope you don't qualify on either front.'

'It's not "help" quite like that. They want me to liaise with you. I was in the police, you know.'

'So you were . . . so you were. And you want my sanction to do the muckracking on old Rees, eh?'

'Not exactly. I could guide them away from treading on too many corns. Sort of diplomatic link.'

'Very well, Philip, you have my blessing. But I want to know exactly what's going on, in writing, every time there's a development. I really don't want to read about Members getting arrested in the papers. I want to know ahead of time. Do you understand?' The Speaker had a reputation for knowing everything that went on in the Commons. He hated being taken by surprise and rarely was. The clerks and his personal staff ensured that the Chair anticipated everything.

'Completely. I thought I'd begin with Mrs Rees.

The police want to interview her this evening.'

'Good grief, I've only just written to her on behalf of the House. She's not a suspect, is she?'

'I really have no idea,' replied North disingenuously. 'But I thought I ought to keep an eye on how the police handle themselves.'

The Speaker rose to his feet. 'Use some tact on this, Philip,' he cautioned. 'Don't drop us all in the cart . . . and keep the police from giving off-the-record briefings to the press. I'm in charge of this investigation, technically, and don't hesitate to remind the police of that fact if the need arises. They're to report to me, and I expect you to make them understand that. This has been a royal palace for a thousand years. They may think it is an anachronism, but it's the law . . . Parliament's law, my responsibility.'

'I quite understand, Mr Speaker,' North added deferentially as the older man swept towards the door.

Just before he left the room he turned briefly. 'Don't let me down, Philip. And if you do, don't expect to be called again in this parliament. Or the next. Or ever.'

Chapter Three

The Opposition Whip

Just after six o'clock North and the two detectives stepped out of Young's Ford Sierra in Lurline Gardens, Battersea, and approached a small semi-detached house near the middle of the quiet tree-lined residential avenue. They had made the journey in good time, considering the rush-hour traffic, but Shawcross had known his south London and deftly manoeuvred the car around the trouble spots. On the way North had explained some of the background to Commons procedure, and the average week of a Member of Parliament. It was, as he described it, not so much a job or a career but a way of life. Not exactly a vocation, but hardly the secure occupation of anyone used to an ordered existence. The Chief Inspector had been anxious to learn about Rees's politics, and discover whether any of his colleagues might have taken their political differences too far. North had assured him, the Speaker's admonition in mind, that a politically motivated attack was quite the most unlikely explanation.

As the trio approached the panelled front door Young stepped forward to press the bell and murmured that he would do the introductions. It was answered by a man in his early fifties, greying at the temples, and evidently very fit.

'Good evening,' said Young. 'Is Mrs Rees at home? I've an appointment to see her. Detective Chief Inspector Young.'

'Please come in,' said the man. 'Mrs Rees will be down in a moment. She's expecting you.'

They were ushered into a respectable-looking sitting-room and settled into the comfortable Dralon-covered chairs surrounding a low coffee table. The man who had come to the door left the room briefly, and was heard calling, 'Sheila . . . the police are here.'

North examined the room. Some tasteless prints on the wall, dozens of framed photographs of grandchildren, and a pile of gardening catalogues and travel guides on the table. While taking in the scene, Sheila Rees came in and closed the door behind her. She looked slightly surprised to see all three men, and her eyes darted nervously over the group. She was a tall, handsome woman, with long dark hair over her shoulders, perhaps in her early forties, North guessed, but very good-looking. She wore beige trousers and an expensive cashmere sweater which showed off her figure. As North admired her, it occurred to him that whoever it was who had opened the front door, and had failed to introduce himself, was much too young to be her father. Her brother perhaps, he wondered.

The senior detective took the initiative. 'Mrs Rees, I'm Detective Chief Inspector Young. We spoke on the phone. I am very grateful to you for seeing me at such short notice, and at this difficult time. You have my sympathy. This is my assistant, Detective Inspector Shawcross, and Mr Philip North, who was one of your husband's colleagues at the Commons. He is accompanying us at the request of the Speaker.'

Sheila Rees shook hands with all three and motioned them to sit down. 'Have you come to tell me that you've found the driver?' she asked. This was the news she had been expecting.

'Not yet. But I'm confident he will be found,' replied Young. 'There is, however, another matter that has arisen. The post-mortem examination has revealed that your husband was being poisoned with a highly toxic substance known as thallium. It is my duty to ask you if you have any knowledge of this.'

'Mr, er . . .' Sheila Rees hesitated. Was she deliberately stalling for time? wondered North.

'Young. The name's Young,' said the detective evenly, watching her intently. He noticed her cheeks flush and North considered whether her reaction was one of shock at hearing the grim news for the first time, or whether she was just angry at the implied accusation. He soon found out.

'Mr Young,' she said angrily, 'you may as well know that I have had very little to do with my husband for the past six months. We were living apart and we were communicating through our solicitors. I have not the slightest idea of what he has been doing, and I know nothing about any poison. We were going to get a divorce.'

'Can you tell me why?' pressed the detective. North could sense the temperature rising uncomfortably and wished the detective would back off.

'I don't really see that it is any of your business, but my husband told me that he was leaving me for someone else.' There was a sharp edge to her voice.

'Do you know who?' asked Young quietly, perhaps warily.

'I have no idea,' flashed the woman, giving the all-too-clear impression to North that she certainly did know. He wondered if the Scotland Yard man was being deliberately obtuse, or whether he had formed the same opinion. In his discomfort North glanced at Mrs Rees who caught his look and seemed to read his mind. 'Of course,' she continued, 'I knew he was keeping some tart in London . . . that was obvious. But I don't know who she is.'

'How long has this been going on?' The detective was not going to be deflected from his task by her undisguised hostility.

'Quite some time, I suppose,' she said a little

absent-mindedly, and not entirely convincingly. 'We met when he was at teacher-training college and I was doing my midwifery exams. We rushed into marriage. We were much too young and after the children were born we just drifted apart. I had no interest whatever in his politics and, to be candid, I was given no choice about living in Cardiff. Frankly, I hate the place.'

'Do you know of any enemies your husband might have had?' probed Young.

Mrs Rees shook her head. 'Not really. We didn't see eye to eye, but I never wished him any harm. He was always involved in controversy, but nothing that would lead anyone to poison him.'

Young switched tack. 'You're staying with your parents here?'

'That's right. I brought the children up from Wales last week.'

'May I ask why?'

'I don't understand your question,' she answered, with a glint of fire in her eyes.

'Well, you were separated from Mr Rees, so why didn't you stay where you were; you came up before he died. What brought you to London?'

'Not another man, if that's what you think,' she said firmly. 'I had agreed to housesit for my parents while they were abroad, and I wanted to get away from Cardiff for a break, that's all. I don't intend to spend the rest of my life in Wales.'

'And where are your parents now?'

'They went the day before yesterday. They'd

booked a trip to Australia to see my uncle a long time ago, and I told them not to cancel because of what had happened. I made them go.'

'And the gentleman who opened the door to us?'

'What about him?' she demanded defensively.

'Can you tell me who he is?' Young had adopted a slightly irritated tone. He was not going to be messed about on a murder inquiry.

'He's just an old family friend. He lives not far away and he's helping out with the children. I asked him over when I knew you were coming. He's very good with them.'

'I see,' said Young. 'And what are your plans now?'

'I'll go back to Wales when my parents return next month, and then I'll have to see. I haven't given much thought to the future. Will I have to give evidence at an inquest or whatever?'

'That's for the coroner to decide but, in the circumstances, I doubt it. However,' he added ominously, 'I may need to see you again.'

'What for?' asked Mrs Rees ungraciously. It was clear that she did not care for Young or his questions.

'I need to know more about your husband.'

What he omitted to mention was the statistical likelihood of murder – at least murder of the white, Anglo-Saxon, northern-European variety – being domestic in nature. In short, Mrs Rees was a suspect.

'But I've already told you. I haven't seen him. I don't know.'

'I understand that. But you must know about his, er, domestic arrangements.' Young was making a weak attempt at being tactful. 'For example, what can you tell me about his secretary?'

'He had two. One in London, part time, whom he shared with another MP. That's Elaine Newman. And there was Gwen Williams at his constituency office in Cardiff. Neither, I can assure you, was his mistress.'

'I'll take your word for it,' smiled Young, pleased for the co-operation. 'Did he have a flat in London?'

'No. He had a room at the National Union of Railwaymen's headquarters in the Euston Road. Several MPs have a London base there.'

'And where did he spend the weekends?'

'Not with me in Cardiff, if that's what you think. He had a room at Paul Skelly's, his constituency agent's house, and I think he used that whenever he had constituency engagements, or attended a General Management Committee meeting.'

'Does Skelly work for him?'

'Oh, no. Paul Skelly is the agent. But he would know much more about Alun's movements than I would.'

'We'll certainly have to talk to him. What about bank accounts?'

'We have a joint account at the building society and a joint mortgage on the house. He has his own account with the Co-op, and I bank with Barclays.'

'Credit cards?'

'A Co-op Visa. He once talked of getting an American Express card, but I don't think he ever did. So much for being a socialist.'

'And who are the solicitors handling his affairs?'

'I assume it's Murray Renshaw Pope, who was dealing with the divorce. They're a local firm in Cardiff.'

'I think that's about everything for the moment.' Young stood up. 'I just need to know, for the record, when you last spoke to your husband.'

'About six weeks ago. I had arranged for him to see the children one Sunday, but at the last moment he rang to say he wouldn't be able to make it.'

'Did he say why?'

'No. But that was not unusual. Not keeping appointments, leaving the family in the lurch. I expect every MP does it. Constituency first, family last. I'd had enough.'

'Thank you for your help, Mrs Rees. One final question . . . a formality really. Can you tell me where you were last Thursday evening . . . between ten and eleven o'clock?'

'I've thought about it quite a lot, Mr Young. I was at the Odeon Leicester Square . . . with a girlfriend.' And for the first time, as she spoke,

North got the strangest feeling that she was lying.

On the way back into the West End, with Shaw-cross at the wheel, North and the senior detective dissected the conversation. 'You could see she loathed Rees. But I don't think him running off with a tart adds up to enough motive for a murder,' opened North.

'I bet she screws like a rattlesnake,' muttered Shawcross under his breath. The Detective Chief Inspector appeared not to hear.

'Our job is simply to get the facts,' said Young. 'A murder investigation is a scientific exercise which accumulates a series of statements which, when a comparison is made, reveals a discrepancy. I don't take anything I am told on face value.'

'So you think she was lying too.'

'I have no doubt. But people lie for a variety of reasons, not just to cover up a murder.'

'Why then?' demanded North.

'Usually for the sake of appearances. Three strange men she has never met before. Awkward personal questions, highly intrusive. It's not like lying on oath, especially if the person concerned is convinced that the issue at hand has no bearing on the murder itself. People lie all the time.'

'And what was she concealing, do you suppose?'

'Perhaps her knowledge of who her husband was having an affair with. To admit she knew, especially to us, would be a rather degrading experience. Imagine the loss of face. She wouldn't want to concede that; nor would she care to reveal that perhaps she had been having an affair too.'

'With the childminder?' asked Shawcross facetiously.

'It wouldn't surprise me. He seemed to know when to make himself scarce,' replied Young. 'I don't think that was the moment to be making demands on her, but we'll have to see her again. Next time we'll ask her to come in to the station.'

'The curious thing is, Chief Inspector, I think I've come across him before. I just can't place his name or face. But I had the distinct impression that I knew him . . . and he knew me. Or knew of me . . . that Welsh accent seemed familiar . . . I shall have to check.'

'Let me know if you come up with anything. In the mean time, I want you to talk to Rees's secretary, Elaine Newman. And if you can spare the time, I would like you to go through Rees's desk and see what he was working on. Anything out of his routine might be useful.'

'And what will you do?'

'We'll have the forensic file tomorrow, but first I'll be taking a look at Rees's room at the union headquarters. Does that sound right . . . that he'd have accommodation there?'

'Some MPs share flats and houses with colleagues, and a few others find digs in Pimlico.

Labour MPs, particularly those sponsored by unions, often get supplied with a room if their headquarters is handy. In much the same way Tories get a room at their club, perhaps the Carlton in St James's Street or St Stephen's which is rather nearer, in Queen Anne's Gate. Those with some money behind them live in the division bell area... that's anywhere within eight minutes of the chamber.'

'Which would exclude the Euston Road.'

'Easily. Otherwise they have to spend more time in the Commons itself. I would guess that most are like me, they have a flat in a mansion block close by, or an apartment in Dolphin Square. Houses just over the river are popular too, but they're very pricey these days.'

'So every MP has to have two homes?'

'That's right. A pied-à-terre in London and a proper home in the constituency. We get a special allowance to cover the extra expense.'

'And does every MP have a mistress as well?'

'Not quite,' North laughed, a little self-consciously and wondered if he sounded a trifle too artificial. 'A popular misconception. We work very odd hours, and we probably spend more time with our secretaries than our wives, which is why there are so many broken marriages. What Mrs Rees told you is painfully familiar. It especially affects those MPs who had been married for some years and only latterly decided to go into politics. It's not always what the wives bargained for.'

'And what's the solution? A vigilant wife?'

'Some refuse to live in the constituency and insist on coming up to London each week with their husbands. They have to be very well organised to manage that kind of régime. Some actually work as their husband's secretary.'

'And get paid by whom?' queried the detective.

'The House of Commons Fees Office. Every MP has an allowance which is just enough to pay a secretary, buy a typewriter and perhaps hire a research assistant. Who he employs is entirely at his discretion. The MP authorises the Fees Office to pay a particular salary scale, and the Serjeant-at Arms issues his nominee with a pass and allocates a room. It's not quite like in the American Senate, where it has always been said that you can tell the member of a Congressman's family on his staff, as she's the ugly one.'

'So we ought to check with the Fees Office to see who Rees was paying?' asked Young, politely ignoring North's levity by making an entry in his notebook.

'I wondered whether you had caught her remark. What was it again? Rees was *keeping* a tart in London. It wasn't that he was *seeing* a tart. He was *keeping* her.'

'That's why I asked about his bank and credit cards. You'd be surprised how easy it is to reconstruct someone's movements from his payment records. I'll also want to see his constituency agent, and it would be helpful if you could sit in on that one too.'

'That'll be quite a novel experience,' murmured North.

'How so?'

'I don't suppose you get many Tory MPs in Labour Party offices, even at the best of times.'

'This'll broaden your horizons then. Now, who else ought we to see in the Commons?'

North pondered the question for a few moments. 'I'll ask around to see who his friends were. You might talk to his whip. Every MP is assigned a particular whip, and Rees would have worked with the regional whip for Wales. And then there are the members he shared his office with. I'll find out their names for you as soon as possible.'

Once North had learned that Rhydian Vaughan was the Welsh whip, he knew exactly where to find him. He was one of those parliamentary stalwarts who seemed to have absolutely no other interest in life, and even resented it when the House went into recess. He ate, lived, slept and breathed the Commons, and as a result he looked permanently unwell. His short, stocky figure, huge beer belly and ruddy bulbous nose made him look as if he was long overdue for his first cardiac arrest. But for all his lack of fitness, he was well regarded by Members on both sides and was eminently approachable.

Quite how much authority he carried as a whip on his own benches was unknown to North, whose own regional whip could get very fierce when the government's majority looked tight for a particular vote and North had, as convention requires, warned his whip that he was not 'sound' on the issue in question. Apart from being the parliamentary party's eyes and ears, sniffing out dissension in the ranks, the whip's job was twofold: to ensure the troops gathered to support the party's policy or, if they were rebellious, to keep them away when the vote was taken. An abstention, though far from ideal, was at least better than a vote with their political opponents. The persuasive power of the whips was legendary and not entirely mythical, for with it came the power of patronage.

Pretend to himself as he might, North was by no means immune to such blandishments, and, with the prospect of escalating private school fees, most of his contemporaries saddled with young families had already made it known that they were available for preferment. But in North's case he had a thriving sideline in an independent video production company that he had started while still at the BBC. Now it had developed into a major concern and, though he occasionally fronted some of the scientific presentations, it made minimal demands on his time, leaving him to pursue issues and causes that caught his interest. For him the offer of the ministerial saloon and surly driver from the Government Car Service was not entirely appealing. Nor would his wife, Cass, have enjoyed their weekends being disturbed by the arrival of the distinctive red dispatch boxes.

North was uncertain how the Opposition whips operated or enforced discipline. Presumably the promise of recognition in a future administration might keep some of the lads in line, but Rhydian Vaughan did not appear, superficially at least, to enjoy the natural authority of some of the Brigade of Guards bluebloods that were his Conservative counterparts. However, what he did have in common with them was his almost continuous presence in the Commons. All whips are obliged to be on the premises, on duty while the House is sitting, ever available to gather intelligence, keep tabs on suspects and attend as many committee meetings as possible. And all with the objective of pushing the government's business through the House with the minimum of delay or, from the other viewpoint, sabotaging ministers and ambushing the other side by calling a division on an obscure item when they least expect it. If there was any gossip around, or any trivia in circulation, a whip was duty-bound to be its receptacle. To admit ignorance of anything was to concede failure. North knew that it was part of the whips' function to gather information and store it away for retrieval at an opportune moment, a little like a Mafia godfather calling in a favour owed, or an intelligence service mobilising a long-dormant sleeper agent. If Rees had had a mistress, or he was financially embarrassed, the whips would know. He might not have known that they knew, but they would anyway. That was their job.

The Housing Corporation was hosting an evening buffet reception beside the river and the National Farmers' Union was running a rival party further along the terrace on House of Lords territory. North calculated that Rhydian Vaughan was likely to be at the buffet. In his experience government-funded quangos were rather freer with the hard liquor than the privately financed bodies which tended to opt for the Commons' own brand of Bulgarian white wine, served at room temperature.

North hovered among the Housing Corporation invitees, feeling mildly conspicuous because he was not wearing one of the obligatory lapel tags which were being issued by a harassed public relations girl at the entrance. He quickly spotted Vaughan, who was attempting to attract the attention of a green-jacketed waiter. North swept a tumbler of whisky off a tray and passed it to Vaughan.

'Ah . . . Philip, isn't it? Most kind. Very thirsty work this housing business, you know.'

'Just wait for the speeches,' replied North with a grin. The older Member looked up sharply.

'Good God, there aren't any, are there?' Like most MPs, he hated having to listen to other people's speeches, particularly if they were of the long, rambling variety, made by men with a mission. On this occasion, the goal would be more public money for more construction projects.

'Don't worry. I'm here to rescue you.'

'At what cost?'

'Nothing more than a colleague's reputation.'

North could see that he suddenly had Vaughan's undivided attention. 'Who?' he asked bluntly.

'Alun Rees.'

'Poor old Alun. You were his pair, weren't you?' It was Vaughan's business to know and approve the pairing arrangements of all his Members.

'He was, and now I'm helping the police investigate his murder. I need your guidance.'

'What do you want to know? I'm assuming anything I tell you will be treated as strictly confidential?'

'Don't worry. You won't read any of it in a newspaper or my memoirs. But we do need to catch a murderer. Anything relevant would help.'

'And has this been cleared by your Chief?' Vaughan was clearly wondering who else was going to learn of this conversation. He knew from his own work that the euphemistically termed 'usual channels' seemed to find out about everything sooner or later.

'This is just between you, me and the police. This won't go through our whips.'

Vaughan looked reassured and took a long draught of whisky. 'You knew Alun's politics: straightforward, and no back-stabbing. Easy to work with and no enemies that I knew of. A hard worker when it suited him, but not wholly popular in the constituency. Good voting record but not a great orator. I don't know why everyone expects every Welsh MP to be able to charm the birds off the trees. Some can, but he couldn't. Good on housing and the environment, but not front-bench material.'

'And talking of birds . . .'

'You have been busy. Yes, his private life was a mess. He had a cow of a wife and I was pleased to learn of their separation.'

'What is her history?'

'It's a familiar story. She was a nurse, or maybe a midwife, I forget which, and Alun developed parliamentary ambitions a little late in the day. She didn't share them. She had been involved with other men and Alun eventually did the sensible thing and found himself a girlfriend.'

'Do you know who?'

'I think she was one of the librarians from the reference room.'

'You mean Alun was having an affair with one of the Commons staff?'

'Don't be so old-fashioned, Philip. It happens all the time here. Surely you know that?'

'Of course. It's just that he didn't really seem the type.'

'Is there such a thing?'

'Perhaps not, on reflection. I must say there's a blonde clerk who works for the Defence Select Committee who has always taken my fancy.

Anyway . . . what about Alun's wife?'

'Sheila was an absolute bitch. Hated politics and hated Alun. Made his life a misery.'

'How so?'

'For a start, her choice in men. It's common knowledge in Cardiff that she had an affair with one of the other men short-listed for the seat.'

'You mean that when Alun was trying to be selected Sheila was involved with one of his opponents?'

'I don't know when it started but that's about the gist of it. The liaison may have begun before the selection process was over, I really don't know. But either way it was . . . unhelpful. She also had a fling with a county councillor. That caused quite a stir too.'

'And Alun knew about these, er, infidelities?'

'He was furious, but they were getting a divorce.'

'I suppose that gives him a motive for murdering her, but not vice versa.'

'I wouldn't put anything past that scheming bitch. She was real trouble. Still, I expect she will attend his funeral as the grief-stricken widow.'

'Did Alun have any other problems . . . perhaps financial?'

'Nothing to do with money, but there was something up to do with the police.'

'Was he under investigation?'

'Nothing quite like that. It was something to do with security.'

'Can you be more specific?'

'I simply don't know, but I will try and find out if you like. The Chief called me in one day and asked me to keep a special eye on Alun as the security people had been asking about him.'

'Rhydian, this could be important. Can you ask him what lay behind his request?'

'I'll find out in the morning and let you know. Anything else?'

'Who else should I talk to about him? Who were his friends in the House?'

'He wasn't much of a mixer . . . not one of those you can always find in Annie's or the Kremlin. Not exactly anti-social, but not one of the lads either. Never likely to get elected on to the National Executive, if you know what I mean. You might try Gwilym Williams or Terry Jones. They knew him as well as anyone on our side. As for yours, you were probably the only Tory he ever spoke to.'

Later that evening North voted in a division called on a money resolution and made his way back to his flat, arriving in time to catch the midnight news. The third item in the bulletin was a story based on a statement from Scotland Yard that following a preliminary investigation into the hit-and-run death of Alun Rees MP last week, a murder inquiry had been set up with an incident room at Rochester Row police station. North was disappointed at the development because although he realised that the news could not have been concealed for much longer, the murderer must now be aware that the hunt was on. Fortunately DCI Young had persuaded the Yard's press office to err on the side of brevity. The statement did not reveal the exact cause of Rees's death, or that the police were looking for up to three killers for the same crime.

Chapter Four

The Secretary

After a hurried breakfast in the Members' Tea-room, congested with the usual Wednesday morning crop of those selected to attend committees, North retraced his steps along the Embankment and then crossed over into Great College Street. Halfway down, on the eastern side, was a large anonymous red-brick building, the Abbey Gardens. This was an overflow to accommodate MPs and their secretaries for whom there was no room in Norman Shaw or the palace itself. After identifying himself to the doorkeeper North was directed to the second floor where he found Elaine Newman waiting for him in what had been Rees's office.

Like most of the Members' rooms, it was sparsely furnished. The Works Department provided standard government-issue utilitarian desk, upright chair, steel filing cabinet and telephone for each Member, but that was the limit. Each room came with an annunciator fixed high on the wall which provided the name of the Member

75

currently addressing the chamber, and a discreet chime signalled when someone else replaced him or her. If the room was big enough there was an allocation of a single armchair, but any other equipment, ranging from typewriters to kettles, had to be supplied out of the Member's own pocket. Some really splashed out and installed a fridge and television, while those with homes near by preferred to work from them. Only senior Members merited a room to themselves. In Rees's case, there were two other desks in the room, and the only non-standard item was a coffee percolator. After North had introduced himself to Rees's secretary he asked who else worked there.

'George Carver is there' – she pointed to the desk beside the window, commanding a view across Westminster School – 'and Terry Latham's there, but he hardly ever comes in. I think he works from his business premises, which are in Victoria somewhere. Can I get you a cup of coffee?'

North accepted the offer. Two mugs were pulled from one of the filing cabinets, and she proceeded to switch on the machine, grind the beans and prepare two filters.

As she made the coffee, North examined Elaine Newman. She was small, but really very attractive. Her short fair hair was held in place by a blue velvet Alice band and her pleated midi-length skirt and patterned shirt did nothing to conceal her trim figure. She was, by Westminster standards, a very good-looking woman, perhaps in her early thirties, and wearing a large diamond engagement ring as well as a gold band on her wedding finger. He turned his attention to what she was saying about Rees's room-mates. Both men were Tories, North remembered. Latham evidently wouldn't be much help but Carver might be. He had been in for a couple of parliaments and was a highly regarded backbencher and an active member of the Trade and Industry Select Committee. If he had spent any time in this room with Rees it was likely that he had acquired a good knowledge of Rees's activities. A few moments later, the coffee was ready.

'As I told you over the telephone,' said North as he sipped his coffee, 'I'm helping the police investigate Alun Rees's murder. What can you tell me about him? Perhaps you could start off with how you met him.'

'I got the job straight after the election. I had been working for Sir Anthony Palmer and Donald Smith in the last parliament but Sir Anthony retired, which left me looking for another MP. I circulated a note to a dozen or so of the new intake, and wound up with Alun.'

'And you still share with Donald Smith?' asked North quietly. He knew Smith only vaguely, a rotund ex-minister with a reputation for alcohol and pretty women. North found himself wondering if Smith had ever tried anything with her.

'Yes. The arrangement works quite well.

Neither can really justify a full-time secretary in London, and they both have, er, had, a secretary in their constituencies.'

'What was your routine with Alun?' North knew that every MP had his or her own idiosyncratic approach to dealing with the never-ending tide of constituency correspondence and the vast mail from lobbyists.

'He collected his own mail from the post office in the Members' Lobby each morning and opened it himself. I start at quarter to nine and we'd do the correspondence together. If he had a committee he would break off the dictation at ten twenty but, depending on his diary, we would clear the decks most days.'

'Whose coffee machine is it?' asked North absent-mindedly.

'That's Alun's. He took his coffee very seriously, an ideologically sound Nicaraguan blend. Politically correct is what they'd call it nowadays. In fact it's very good, but he was a real coffee snob. He almost had withdrawal symptoms if he didn't have three strong shots of caffeine during the morning. It was my first duty every day . . . it helped him get through the tedium of his post.'

'And where is your office?' It was the exception rather than the rule for MPs to be allocated offices in the same building as the secretary. It was almost as though the Palace of Westminster had been deliberately designed to create administrative chaos.

'In Old Palace Yard. Don Smith is a barrister so we tend to work together in the afternoons, usually after Questions.'

'And did you answer Alun's telephone?' Some MPs preferred to have their calls filtered so as to avoid the pollsters and time-wasters.

'No. When he wasn't in his office he diverted his calls through to the answering service. If he didn't get the messages straight away they came in the mail each morning.'

'And his private correspondence: bills, letters, things of that kind?'

'He did all that himself from home. I never saw any of that at all.'

'What about his family?'

'I never met them. He occasionally mentioned his children' – she pointed to two framed photographs on what had been Rees's desk – 'but he never said anything about his wife, apart from the fact that she was in Cardiff and rarely came up to London.'

'What did you make of that?' North was fishing for anything that could provide a motive.

'I guessed they had separated, or were about to. It's not a novelty around here, as you must know.'

'Excuse me for asking, but did he ever tell you he was seeing anyone else?'

'Certainly not,' she replied primly.

'Are you quite sure? I had heard he had been seeing one of the librarians?'

'I never heard that, but he once asked me out,' she admitted, perhaps a little reluctantly, North thought.

'What happened?'

'Nothing, of course,' she replied, somewhat unconvincingly. 'It was some Welsh dinner in London and I turned him down flat. Quite apart from what my husband would say, I'm not of Alun's political persuasion and this is a job for me, nothing more.'

'Since you mention your husband,' said North, taking the opportunity to pry a little further, 'can you tell me what he does?'

'Mark works in the City ... at Lloyd's actually.'

'Thanks,' said North, making a discreet note on his pad. 'Now, getting back to Alun ... did he have any nutters to deal with, any threats?'

'We have a couple of strange ladies. One is pursuing a long-standing vendetta against the Inland Revenue and the other is always suing solicitors. Then we have the usual, you know, the cheated pools winners, the victim of police injustice, and a publican who got nasty and accused Alun of conspiring to have his licence taken away.'

'But none who posed a serious threat to Alun?' They sounded very familiar to North, who had his own share of disorientated spinsters and aggrieved citizens convinced the authorities had plotted against them. Few were really dangerous, but who could tell?

'None that I knew about,' said Elaine.

'What was he working on when he died?' pressed North.

'He was on the committee of an environmental bill and he was campaigning for the closure of a recycling plant in the constituency. There were other things as well, but he spent most of his time on the bill, tabling amendments and making a nuisance of himself.'

'Any local opposition to him?' North was interested in any internal party strife or faction-fighting in the constituency. Taking on a big employer locally would be a guaranteed source of controversy.

'Oh, yes. The union was completely split. Paul Skelly could tell you all about that. One group wanted to keep the jobs, but some of the process workers thought their health might be damaged. We had to deal with a lot of scientific evidence about the disposal of toxins. We received research material from some of the national pressure groups who had become involved after Alun had approached them, and there was a fair amount of library work for him.'

'Did he get any help?' North was on another fishing expedition.

'He enjoyed doing the research himself,' replied Elaine, apparently not responding to the bait. 'He had an academic background and I think he was too mean to employ a research assistant.'

'How did the company react to Alun's campaigning?'

'It was very hostile and solicitors' letters had been flying, but Alun knew enough about parliamentary procedure to be protected.'

'How serious was it?'

'Alun had tabled an Early Day Motion criticising the company's record and they weren't pleased. They sent him a very stroppy note threatening all kinds of litigation.'

'How did Alun respond?' North knew that every MP was protected by the ancient tradition of parliamentary privilege which shielded them from the usual legal consequences of defamation.

'Alun went straight to the Clerk of the Committee of Privileges. The company backed down when they realised they had overstepped the mark.'

'Any other hot issues?' asked North while making another note on his pad.

'Paul Skelly, the agent in Cardiff, probably knows better than me, but as far as I'm concerned there was only one worth mentioning. Alun had got mixed up with a weirdo, a man who had been with the SAS, or so he claimed. Said he wanted to tell Alun all about dirty tricks in Northern Ireland. I think he was a Walter Mitty, but Alun wasn't so sure. Alun could be a little naïve ... even gullible sometimes. Donald Smith tosses letters like that straight into the bin.'

'Did you tell Alun this?'

'Certainly not. I take dictation, type letters, and leave them for my Member to sign and post. It would have been quite impertinent for me to offer him gratuitous advice. I might have told him if he had asked me for my opinion, but he never did. We didn't have that kind of relationship.'

'So did you actively disapprove of his letters?' North thought he could detect an element of scorn in her voice.

'Sometimes. He was always trying to get union sponsorships, and all these begging letters would go out, but I made sure he paid for the postage. He never abused the pre-paid envelopes.' As North knew to his cost, the Serjeant-at-Arms took an uncompromising view of the sanctity of the free envelopes.

'Do you have a record of the SAS man's name and address?' asked North.

'We kept a monthly day file with photocopies of all letters, and I have an index on my computer of each addressee. I can certainly look him up and let you have his address once I get his name from the day file.'

'And where is that?'

'I don't know. I rather thought the police must have it. We kept it in this drawer' – she opened the lower of the two desk drawers – 'but it hasn't been here for several days.'

'But you have a duplicate on your computer?'

'Not exactly. Alun would dictate a standard letter on each topic as it arose, and I would print up each reply as it was needed. Alun would top and tail it, and I kept a record of the addressee on the computer with a Xerox of every individual reply in the day file. There was no point in maintaining a copy on disc of every letter because so many are the same. The volume is so huge ... we're talking about two hundred letters a week when the animal rights activists and the anti-abortion campaigners get into gear.'

'Not to mention the Sunday-opening reformers,' muttered North.

'Exactly. Your mailbag must be much the same.'

'So without Alun's day file you would have to trawl through your address list to identify the SAS man.'

'That's right,' she agreed. 'At any one time Alun probably had fifty cases pending. Most are Social Security queries which get referred to the local office for settlement or, if they involve a matter of principle, straight to the department for ministerial review. Then there are the county and district council issues which are delegated to the relevant councillor. That leaves a handful of authentic problems for the Member to take up personally. When you analyse Alun's, they both boil down to our regular customers, who can be discounted for your purposes, current or imminent legislation, coastal protection for the dolphins, the recycling plant and an SAS fantasist.'

'So in your view Alun's murder was not connected to his work in the Commons?' concluded North.

'Judge for yourself,' she replied. 'None of them strikes me as very promising.'

'One final thing,' added North. 'The police want a schedule of Alun's movements during the week before his death. Did you keep an office diary for him?'

'No, he kept his own appointments book, but if I had the correspondence file I could duplicate his engagements quite easily. All invitations went into the front of the folder, in chronological order.'

'So that missing file also holds the key to where Alun was every day?' said North.

'That and his pocket diary which he kept on him. I'll see what I have on the computer that might be relevant.'

North had been inclined to agree with the proposition that Alun Rees's murder was not directly linked to his work in the Commons. Even the most ruthless of multinationals was unlikely to resort to hiring a hitman because an MP was creating a fuss over a controversial site. The chemical industry was well used to defending itself against environmental activists and even the cowboys had learned that what was euphemistically known as 'direct action' was ultimately counter-productive and only served to attract even greater media interest. Which left some improbable candidates for involvement in murder: the same eccentric spinsters who routinely dominated much of the daily post, a nutcase overreacting to some piece of legislation before the House, or a familiar-sounding psychiatric outpatient who had invented a past for himself in the Special Air Service Regiment. In North's experience such characters sounded perfectly sane until they mentioned receiving signals from extra-terrestrials or television sets. At least this particular tale made a change from the more common paranoia of being on the run from MI5. As he explained to Detective Chief Inspector Young when they met later the same morning, none of Rees's parliamentary cases was very promising as a motive for murder.

'It's a little strange that Rees's correspondence file, with copies of all his current letters, should go missing just now,' said North, 'but there may be an innocent explanation. It shouldn't make a lot of difference because Mrs Newman has a complete record on her computer of everyone Rees wrote to. It may just take a little longer to match up the names and addresses, and there may be a delay in identifying his SAS man. But from what I have seen so far, there's nothing sinister in any of his parliamentary work.'

'Which leaves his private life,' said Young. 'We've checked his room in the railwaymen's headquarters. It was hardly used and there were virtually no possessions there. I think he was living somewhere else. Did his secretary have any ideas?'

'It certainly wasn't with her,' answered North.

'She says he asked her out once, but she had made it clear she wasn't going to mix business with pleasure. Anyway she wasn't his type.'

'Which is . . . ?' quizzed Young, stroking his chin.

'Whatever it was, it isn't her. She's a Sloane Ranger with a husband in the City. They couldn't be more different.'

'So we have an elusive mistress, no idea where Rees was living, and only an embittered wife with medical training and a motive.'

'What motive?' asked North. 'I thought we had agreed that he was the wronged party in the marriage?'

'Maybe, but we've been on to his solicitors. He left no will that they know of, which means he was intestate.'

'So she stands to inherit,' murmured North.

'Quite,' agreed the detective.

'But what does that amount to? Half a house in Cardiff? Hardly worth killing for, surely?' asked the MP sceptically.

'Well, according to his solicitors, there was rather more to it than that. It seems that his uncle died in February and left Rees a sizable farm in Pembrokeshire. Your late pair was on the verge of becoming a millionaire.'

North gave a low whistle. 'He kept pretty quiet about that. The newspapers would have had a field day if they'd found out.'

'This makes Sheila Rees our best suspect.

Whether she is the poisoner, the hit-and-run driver or the Semtex bomber, or even all three, remains to be seen. Shawcross is down in Wales now and will attend the funeral this afternoon. The local CID will photograph and identify all the mourners, and I'm going to interview Skelly, Rees's agent in the morning.'

'You're going down to Cardiff?' asked North.

'No. Apparently he had to come up to London tomorrow anyway,' explained Young.

'That would figure. With a by-election pending the Labour Party's national headquarters would want to confer with the agent.'

'He's coming here, to Rochester Row, at ten, if you'd like to be there.' North nodded to indicate he would. 'Anything else to report?' Young asked.

'Yes, something Rees's regional whip brought up. Apparently he had been tipped off that the security authorities had expressed an interest in Rees.'

'What sort of security? Special Branch or MI5?'

'He didn't know. He'd been asked by the Opposition Chief Whip to keep an eye on Rees and he's going to find out more today.'

'That's interesting. Of course we've done a routine check on Rees with Criminal Records and the collator in Cardiff but there's nothing known apart from two traffic offences.'

'That showed up on the Police National Computer?'

'No, the Drivers and Vehicle Licensing Agency

at Swansea. We had to do a check on his car and it turns out that Rees's licence had been endorsed twice for speeding in Wiltshire.'

'Probably the M4. The motorway police used to be very hot on that stretch.' North omitted to add that he knew this to his cost, having once been banned for three months by Trowbridge magistrates. 'And speaking of Rees's car, there's something that's been troubling me about the bomb.'

'What in particular?'

'Ever since Airey Neave was assassinated by the Irish National Liberation Army all vehicles coming into New Palace Yard have been checked at the security post. There are two men there night and day, and they examine every car. They're very thorough.' North could see that Young was suddenly very alert.

'When you say every car, do you mean MPs as well as visitors?'

'There aren't any visitors' cars admitted to New Palace Yard. They're stopped at the gate by the police and directed to St Stephen's entrance. The only cars allowed through are those belonging to Members, and they have to display a special pass to get past the security barrier on the ramp into the underground carpark. They are physically searched by the guards who even look under the vehicle with mirrors.'

'So it would be impossible for a car to enter the garage with a bomb under the wheel-arch?' asked the detective thoughtfully.

'I doubt it. You see the terrorists fitted Airey Neave's car with a mercury detonator outside his flat. Nothing happened when he started the engine, or when he drove to the Commons. He even survived when he went *down* into the car-park. But when he drove out, the bomb went off at the steepest point of the upwards incline. The tilt mechanism worked in one direction and not the other.'

'So since Neave's assassination what you really mean is that Rees's bomb was more likely to have been fitted to his car *in* the garage than outside,' murmured Young.

'In a nutshell, yes,' agreed North.

'And is access to it restricted to Members only?' asked the more senior detective.

'Oh, no. The lower level is reserved for the senior clerks, and anyone with an identity card could get in there.'

'Are there any security barriers between the garage and the rest of the building?'

'None. There is a security guard on duty at the vehicle entrance to check the windshield passes on the cars, and ensure that the drivers hold an ID card, but the pedestrian access is completely unrestricted. A bank of three lifts and a separate staircase serve all the levels and bring the drivers to a lobby under the Members' Entrance in New Palace Yard. An escalator then carries them to the surface where there are two exits. One door-way leads into an inner courtyard and is used by most of the palace staff. The other is mainly for Members and emerges by the Members' cloakroom.'

'So although access down the ramp is restricted, almost anyone could get in by foot using the pedestrian entrance?'

'It would assume some local knowledge on the part of the person involved but if someone, perhaps even a visitor, had already got into the main building they might be able to make their way to the carpark lifts without being challenged.'

'But surely the police patrol the corridors and would challenge an unknown face?'

'Quite probably. All I'm saying is that there's a very strong chance the bomb was placed on Rees's car *after* he had parked it in the garage.'

'Accepting your scenario for a moment, how would a terrorist know where Rees had parked his car? Is each Member allocated a particular space?'

'No. The car pass entitles the car to be parked in the garage, and most Members try to find a space as close to the surface as possible, but on busy days when most have been taken one has to go right to the bottom. It just means a little further to walk, that's all.'

'But that presents a formidable obstacle for the would-be terrorist, who has carried his bomb into the main building and managed to smuggle it past the security checkpoints. Even if he gets it as far as the garage, he won't know where Rees's car is parked. It might take him hours to find it. That place is enormous and holds, what . . . a thousand cars?'

'Enough for six hundred and fifty Members, I guess,' replied North.

'And the clerks as well. And anyway, how would the terrorist know that Rees had even brought his car into the garage? He might have parked elsewhere. Don't Members with offices at the Abbey Gardens have their own carpark there?'

'That's true,' conceded North. 'All of which makes one think that Rees's car was selected at random. A terrorist carried the bomb into the garage, and then placed it on the first car he saw.'

'Well, that won't wash either,' remarked Young. 'Rees's car was parked some distance from the pedestrian access on that level, and there were quite a few other cars around, closer to hand. And there were some much more expensive cars too. No, someone specifically selected Rees's car. The question is, why?'

'And who? Are there any clues in the forensic report?' North asked.

'Which one? This is the first murder I've ever come across where there are three, each apparently conflicting with the next. The Anti-Terrorist Branch have given me a detailed brief on the bomb. The Semtex was manufactured in Czechoslovakia and its most likely route to Britain was courtesy of the Libyans who bought tons of the stuff and then donated it to Colonel Gadaffi's favoured causes. That includes the PLO, the French *Action Directe*, the German Red Army Faction, the Italian Red Brigade, the Provisional IRA and the Basque ETA movement. And there were plenty of others too.'

'What about the Welsh nationalists?'

'Them too. The Sons of Owen Glendower, as I've already mentioned. But according to the Special Branch they're more on the other extreme: right-wing separatists rather than international socialists of the left.'

'Does it make a difference?'

'Perhaps not. Semtex is legitimately used for blasting, and it would be easy enough for a quantity to be stolen from a mine or a quarry.'

'Of which there are plenty in Wales.'

'Too true. Then I've got a file from the Home Office laboratory on thallium, which is a metallic compound, and one of the most toxic substances known to man. Not easy to get hold of, and is not refined at all in this country. However, it is a by-product of some chemical processes and quite lethal. The effect of small doses is cumulative and ultimately fatal. There is only one real expert on the substance in this country, and that's my namesake, Graham Young.'

'Was he the St Albans poisoner?' queried North. 'I think I recall the case.'

'He bumped off most of his family and then set to work on his factory colleagues. Quite a handful died before he was eventually caught. We can rule him out as he's still in prison. Generally, though, poison tends to be more a woman's method.'

'But Sheila Rees would hardly have access to either Semtex or thallium,' objected North.

'Which leaves her as a candidate for the hit-and-run artist,' said Young bluntly. 'Hardly a classic female crime, but she might have slipped away from the cinema and driven to Westminster. It's quite a coincidence that she happened to be within a mile of where her husband was murdered . . . and she had the medical training.'

'But if Sheila Rees drove the car, who was on hand to finish off her husband with pressure on his carotid artery? She couldn't have done both.'

'A boyfriend?' speculated North.

'Perhaps Shawcross will make better progress in Wales on that score,' said Young. 'He's going to make a few inquiries into her background while he's there for the funeral. Let me know if anything else comes to mind. Otherwise I'll see you tomorrow morning with Skelly.'

North returned to his room at Norman Shaw where he found his own secretary, Belinda, ploughing through a pile of letters. She was a recent acquisition, a temporary replacement for his regular, Camilla Ponsonby, who had left to have her baby. North prayed for her quick return, for Belinda had never worked for an MP before, and was quite unused to the strange hours and cramped working conditions.

'There's nothing urgent, Philip, but I think the library must have made a mistake. There's a whole lot of Early Day Motions and extracts from *Hansard*, but they're all to do with that chap who was run over last week.'

'That's all right, Belinda. I asked the library to fish it all out for me. There should be something from the Fees Office about him too.'

'There is. It's a copy of his office and secretarial allowance statement. That's a bit personal, isn't it?'

'Don't worry,' he replied. 'I'm doing it for the police. Rees was murdered.'

'I know. It's in all the papers this morning.'

'Did you know him?'

'Frankly, I'd never even heard of him.'

'What about his secretary, Elaine Newman. Have you come across her?'

'I don't think so. Listen, I've got to dash for lunch. I'm meeting someone in Beauchamp Place. Would you mind awfully if we did all this later on?'

North smiled indulgently and let her go. As there was nothing urgent in his mailbag he preferred to concentrate on Rees, and the material the library had gathered for him. During the following two hours he absorbed himself in every Early Day Motion signed by Rees during the past twelve months, and read the whole of the Private

Members' Bill on protecting dolphins that Rees had sponsored. North suspected that DCI Young was now disinclined to pursue the parliamentary angles to his investigation, convinced that Rees's occupation was largely immaterial. North was not so sure.

The EDMs were excruciatingly boring, and none seemed sufficiently provocative to risk physical violence. EDMs had been greatly devalued in recent years when more and more Members used them as a vehicle to criticise government policy. Theoretically, a well-supported EDM, with hundreds of MPs' signatures, might prompt some action at the end of the parliamentary year, but the reality was that they were nothing more than a means of bringing an issue to the fore by having the text published on the order paper. Every time a Member added his signature the entire document would be reprinted. Most were on relatively trivial topics, and had probably only been signed by the Members concerned in response to a request from an awkward constituent, but there was one series in the pile that caught North's eye. Its subject was a Labour Party favourite, tax evasion and fraud in the City, and over a period of months Rees had supported the same dozen or so Opposition colleagues who were calling for a public inquiry. What intrigued North was the persistence with which a particular underwriting syndicate, Peter Cameron Webb, had been singled out for special attention. On a hunch, North reached for the telephone and put a call through to Lloyd's.

'Can you put me through to the Cameron Webb syndicate, please?' he asked the switchboard operator.

'I'm sorry, PCW is no longer in the market,' she replied, 'but I can put you through to the managing agents who are working off the account if you wish.'

'Thank you,' replied North, and waited a few moments to hear another operator answer, 'Colby Foreman.'

'Is your firm handling PCW inquiries?' asked North.

'I'm afraid so,' said an anonymous voice. 'How can we help you?'

'Do you have a Mr Mark Newman working for you?'

'We certainly do. Would you like to speak to him?'

'No, that's fine, thank you.' He hung up slowly, wondering why Elaine Newman had not mentioned that Rees had been in pursuit, indirectly, of her husband. She must have known of his EDMs, as his signature appeared on about ten of them naming PCW. Indeed, Mark Newman must have known of Rees's interest in him, and presumably that his wife was Rees's secretary. North wondered if the pretty Mrs Newman had told her husband that Rees had made a pass at her . . . if that was what it had been.

He stored away the information in his mind and turned to the next item in the dossier compiled by the Commons library. It was an extract from *Parliamentary Profiles*, a slightly scurrilous reference book which offered pen-portraits of all current MPs. Written by an American with strong leftist credentials who had been observing the Commons for more than forty years, what *Profiles* contained often bordered on the actionable and its author had once been sued for defamation, to his considerable cost, by Harold Wilson. But there was nothing libellous in the short entry that Rees merited. It described him cruelly, but perhaps not inaccurately, as 'an inarticulate soft-left bore with academic pretensions'. It was safe to assume that if *Profiles* had been so uncharacteristically restrained and inoffensive, there would be little in the newspaper cuttings to Rees's detriment. As a rule the book faithfully reproduced any derogatory newspaper gossip, no matter how ill-informed. Instead it seemed to bear a marked similarity to Rees's bland entry in *Who's Who*.

The next Xerox sheet in the envelope from the highly efficient Commons reference library was a page from the current *Who's Who*. He knew that he had recognised the man at Sheila Rees's house in Wandsworth, but he had been unable to place his face and voice, both of which had been familiar. Then, in conversation with Rhydian Vaughan, it had dawned on him who the man

might have been: Neil Roberts . . . the sitting MP
Alun Rees had beaten at reselection for his Cardiff seat, and the man Sheila had been involved
with. Had been? North wondered about the past
tense. Now, according to *Who's Who*, which listed
all past as well as current MPs, he had an address
in Battersea and was on the board of the Welsh
Industrial Development Agency. North continued
to scan the page. Roberts had read economics at
Aberystwyth University, was apparently still
married, but had no children. He had listed his
recreations as reading, opera and hill-walking.

Finally, North sifted through the computer
print-out from the Fees Office. It gave a current
summary of Rees's travel expenses, his subsist-
ence payments, and a statement of his office and
secretarial allowance. The latter was of particular interest, for although it showed that Elaine
Newman was being paid the going rate, nine
thousand a year for a shared, part-time secretary,
it revealed that more than half that much again
was going to a research assistant named Gail
Crosby with an address in St George's Square,
SW1. No further details were listed, not even a
National Insurance number.

'Bingo,' muttered North out loud as he reread
the computer sheet. 'So Alun had no research
help, eh? Enter one mistress . . . paid for by the
tax-payer.'

Chapter Five

The Mistress

Shortly before slipping into the chamber while Foreign Office Questions were still in progress, North grabbed a sandwich for a belated lunch in the Members' Tearoom. Then he headed down to the Members' Entrance on New Palace Yard where he collected a cab. He knew there was no division scheduled on the Scottish Transport Bill until seven and gave the driver Gail Crosby's address in St George's Square.

Within ten minutes North had paid off the taxi and was standing outside one of the large, once-elegant houses on the west side of the square. Only a few of the houses remained entirely in private hands. Most had been turned into low-cost hotels or bedsits. North checked the six names on the entryphone and then descended the steps to the basement. A single bell was marked 'Crosby', and he rang it. He noticed a net curtain move slightly in the barred window, and moments later the panelled door was opened on a security chain. 'Yes?' asked a woman's voice, with a slight transatlantic accent.

'Miss Crosby? My name is Philip North. I was one of Alun Rees's colleagues. I need to speak to you about him.' His tone was deliberately soft and confiding, almost conspiratorial, in the hope that she would trust him enough to let him in.

'I don't know what you mean,' the voice replied ambiguously. North wasn't sure whether the woman was denying being Gail Crosby, or pretending not to know Rees.

'I'm helping the police investigate his death. If you don't talk to me, you'll have to talk to them. It's up to you.' The threat was unmistakable, or so he intended.

There was another few moments' hesitation, and then the door was closed while the chain was removed. When the door opened he saw a short, rather dishevelled woman in her late twenties motioning him inside. North could see she had been crying.

'I'm sorry,' she apologised, 'but I have to be so careful. Of course, I recognise you now. You used to do those science programmes on the television, didn't you?'

'That's right,' replied North. 'I hope I didn't scare you. I wanted to call first but your number is ex-directory.' He mentioned the fact in the expectation that she would offer an explanation, but she ignored the invitation.

'I'm not sure I understand,' she said. 'Why do you want to talk to me?'

'Because you worked for Alun,' replied North. It was as though she was on the point of breaking down, or perhaps about to deny ever having known him. She was watching him intently.

'You'd better come in,' she said quietly. 'How did you find me?'

North looked around the room he had been shown into. It was a large, low-ceilinged sitting-room decorated with what looked like good prints on the walls. Newspapers were scattered across the sofa and a solid oak table. The whole of one wall was covered with a stripped pine bookcase, packed with textbooks and files. At the other end of the room an angled lamp was switched on, bathing a small upright desk in light. The curtains at the rear of the room were still drawn and there was a faint smell of cats. As he took in the surroundings North explained his presence. 'It wasn't easy,' he acknowledged. 'Alun's secretary didn't know he also had a research assistant, but the Fees Office have a record of your salary, and your mailing address. Unfortunately they didn't have your telephone number as well.'

Gail Crosby put on a pair of glasses and started to tidy some of the papers covering the sofa. 'Please do have a seat. I'm sorry about the mess but it's difficult to keep the place tidy, especially when I'm working. It's all been rather a ghastly shock. Sometimes I think I might be dreaming this whole nightmare.'

'You worked for Alun,' said North again, more

as a statement than a question.

'Yes. Isn't that why you're here?' she said defensively.

'Indeed. Yet Elaine Newman didn't seem to know that he had hired a research assistant. Now that's a little . . . odd.' North had searched for the right word to use. Gail Crosby was so different to the other two women in Rees's life. Sheila Rees was so confident, so capable. Elaine Newman had been clinically efficient, but still very attractive. And here was a vulnerable, mousy girl, a complete contrast to Rees's wife and secretary. He sensed that, however improbably, she had indeed been Rees's mistress.

'That was Alun's decision,' said Gail, as though she had not been a party to it, and perhaps had not even been consulted. 'He didn't really trust her. She was obviously a Tory and Alun suspected she would leak some of his more sensitive work to the government.'

'What sort of work?' asked North quietly. It seemed unlikely to him that Rees had ever dealt with anything that could justifiably be described as that important.

'I'm not sure if I should tell you.' She hesitated. 'If Alun really was murdered, as the papers say, I think he may have been the victim of an assassination. The work he was doing was terribly controversial, you see.'

'Anything you tell me will be treated as confidential,' said North, scarcely believing that Rees could have had access to anything remotely secret. 'I am here on the Speaker's authority, and you can tell me anything. I promise that you won't come to any harm. And the information may well lead us to Alun's killer. Now, what was he working on that you say put him in danger?'

'Alun was preparing a case against a minister. He thought it might bring the government down.'

'A cabinet minister?' asked North sceptically. How could a rather lacklustre Opposition back-bencher like Rees threaten the government's survival? Perhaps Rees had been indulging in a little self-aggrandisement to impress this woman. For a moment he wondered if she knew the difference between a secretary of state and the more junior minister of state.

'Not quite,' she conceded, 'but a senior minister all the same.'

'Can you tell me who?' pressed North.

'Roland Wells,' she said firmly, almost as an accusation.

North thought carefully about the revelation. Roland Wells was an ambitious minister of state in the Department of Trade and Industry who had been promoted in the last reshuffle after a two-year stint in Northern Ireland. A scandal involving him would certainly embarrass the government, but it would hardly make it fall. His suspicion that Rees had exaggerated the significance of Wells seemed well founded. 'What had Alun got on Wells?'

'We knew that Wells had been the victim of a blackmail racket—'

'Steady on,' said North. 'Not so fast. Why was he being blackmailed? Who told Alun? You'd better start from the beginning.'

Gail Crosby accepted the instruction without demur. 'Alun was tipped off by a former soldier who had been involved in intelligence operations in Ulster. Wells is gay, and had been caught on camera in a surveillance operation while he was a minister at Stormont Castle. He had picked up a young lad in Belfast but had not realised that the whole thing had been a set-up.'

'Was the operation mounted specifically to catch him?' asked North, his throat beginning to dry up. This was serious.

'Oh, no,' said Gail confidently. 'They'd been after Unionists. Wells had simply blundered in, and had then been filmed in action.'

'And who was running this? Who are "they"?' North realised that if this was true it probably did constitute a major scandal.

'According to Alun's informant it had been a deniable project mounted by MI6. But instead of reporting what had happened, the person responsible for looking after the equipment had pocketed the videotape and then blackmailed Wells.'

North sat back to take stock. It was not impossible that Wells was gay, but it seemed incredible that a homosexual in his position would even attempt to get involved in something of this kind . . . and in Northern Ireland of all places. It was an unpopular posting for obvious reasons, particularly among ministers with families, which was perhaps why Wells, who was a bachelor, had stayed there so long. Among his colleagues he was held in high regard, and his switch to the Department of Trade had been widely tipped and fully deserved in the opinion of most commentators. As for the part about the deniable operation, it was probably true that some of the intelligence agencies operating in Ulster had indulged in such tactics. But for a renegade to try and put pressure on a serving minister, that was . . . dynamite.

'Did Alun have any proof of these allegations?' Without proof, North knew, such tales would be dismissed as mere mischief-making by one side or the other of the sectarian divide in Ulster, of the kind familiar to every journalist who had served in the province.

'That's what he was working on. But you haven't heard the full story. Alun's source said that the blackmail had only started quite recently, and involved a reinsurance fraud. Wells was supposedly being forced to block an investigation into a syndicate that had been siphoning off money from Lloyd's.'

'So this wasn't blackmail for money?' With none of the usual motives North feared that the scandal might prove uncontainable. How could an Irish sectarian matter be mixed up with insurance?

'Oh, no. Money wasn't involved. Alun would

have gone straight to Wells, or maybe the police if that had been the case. This was political blackmail. Corruption,' she added with a hint of triumph.

So this was nothing to do with the paramilitaries in Belfast, thought North. It was a City scandal. 'And the Lloyd's syndicate; it wasn't PCW by any chance?'

'So you *do* know about it?' challenged Gail.

North shook his head. 'Hardly. I know that Alun was one of several Opposition MPs who had signed EDMs pressing for an inquiry into City fraud and, in particular, this insurance syndicate. I was putting two and two together.'

Gail appeared to accept his explanation. 'Alun reckoned that if Wells refused the Opposition's demand for a full-scale independent inquiry, headed by a DTI inspector, it would confirm that Wells had been got at.'

'So there's no real evidence that any of the story about blackmail was even remotely true?' North was determined to uncover the extent of Wells's exposure, almost as though he was acting as counsel for Wells's defence.

'We were checking out the source.' She used the jargon confidently, as though she had attended the Woodward and Bernstein school of journalism. 'He had been in Northern Ireland at the time he claimed to be, and he had been part of an intelligence unit there.'

'But not MI6?' queried North.

'He never said he was in MI6. He said that he had been in the SAS, and that he knew the person who had pocketed the compromising tape of Wells and the boy. He said that the MI6 man had also once been in the SAS, and they had both served together.'

'And how did the Lloyd's syndicate become involved?' asked the MP. This particular conspiracy sounded a little too labyrinthine for his taste.

'I'm not sure. Alun was going to get the details, and I think he had set up a meeting the night he was murdered.'

'You don't know?' asked North, adopting his role as a courtroom advocate.

'Alun was very protective towards me,' she explained. 'He didn't want to put me in any danger and he knew there was some risk involved in this business. I had to research all the City end, but he kept me away from his contact. As it happened, I knew he had fixed a confidential appointment soon after the ten o'clock division on Thursday. I suppose they were going to have a drink together and the SAS man was going to tell Alun everything.'

'And as far as you know that meeting happened?' North cast his mind back to their encounter in the Kremlin and wondered whether Rees had been in any condition to meet a contact. Perhaps nerves had made him drink too much.

'I'm really not sure. First there was the

accident, and now the news that Alun had been murdered.'

'But as far as you know, there are two quite separate issues here: an allegation that Wells had been videotaped in Northern Ireland . . . and then a story that Wells had been approached to shelve the investigation into the reinsurance fraud.' North needed more answers before he could begin to make any sense of the situation.

'The SAS man said he could prove a link between the two.' Clearly Gail believed in it, and wanted it to be true.

'Who was he? What is his name?' asked North quietly.

'Alun's source? I didn't know his name but I think there was a Welsh connection. Alun knew because he had checked and established that the man had indeed been in the SAS in Northern Ireland as he had claimed.'

'How did the SAS man get in touch with Alun originally?' North's mind was racing ahead, contemplating the obstacles that would be placed in his way of tracing Army personnel who had served in Ulster. Even the Speaker would get no help from the Ministry of Defence unless he gave a pretty good reason. And digging up dirt on a minister hardly qualified in that category.

'It was all very mysterious,' she said. 'He wrote to Alun saying he had to speak to him on an important matter, and intended to telephone Alun at the Commons each morning at nine thirty until he reached him. He also claimed that the entire matter was strictly secret and lives were at risk. I don't know what happened when they spoke, but Alun agreed to see him and arranged an appointment. He had said it was to do with PCW. Alun could hardly have turned him down.'

'If this was all so secret, why had Alun told you as much as he evidently has?' He wondered if she might take this opportunity to elaborate on the nature of their relationship, whatever it was.

'Alun used me to research PCW. I've been working on this fraud case for six months.'

'How had that happened?' The idea of assigning a single issue to an assistant to study for months at a time was an extraordinary luxury, quite outside North's parliamentary experience. He wondered how Rees could have set it all up – never mind find somebody willing to help him.

Gail volunteered the explanation. 'My fiancé was one of those who had been cleaned out by PCW. He lost everything, and eventually took an overdose. He had been suffering from depression anyway, and I knew the symptoms, but the prospect of bankruptcy utterly destroyed him. After that, I wrote to various MPs to get them to take an interest in what had happened.'

'And Rees was one of those who responded positively?'

'Not exactly. Gwilym Williams had agreed to see me, and he introduced me to Alun. We got talking . . . and Alun offered to help.' Whilst moments earlier she had exuded confidence at the idea of embroiling a minister in a sordid episode of blackmail, now she seemed terribly naïve, seeking help from Rees without realising how he might take advantage of her.

'And did he live here too?' North judged that it was the right time to start asking the more awkward questions. He felt he had gained her trust.

Gail Crosby let out a long sigh, took off her glasses and North could see that her eyes were spilling tears. 'I don't really expect you to understand, but we loved each other.'

'And why wouldn't I understand that?' asked North quietly.

'You're all so . . . unsympathetic. When I wrote to six MPs to tell them about PCW I wrote to three Labour Members and three Tories. Two of the Tories didn't even bother to reply, and I later discovered that both were Names at Lloyd's. They had an interest in keeping this matter covered up. Do you realise how many Tory MPs are members of Lloyd's?'

North ignored the question. Under other circumstances he would have pointed out that City interests such as Lloyd's are all publicly available from the Register of Members' Interests. 'How did you choose which MPs to approach?'

'I just wrote to members of the Trade and Industry Select Committee. Perhaps I was a little . . .

untutored then, but I thought it was their job to investigate matters like this. Anyway, Mr Williams was very sweet.'

'Was one of the Conservative Members George Carver?' asked North, concerned that there might be aspects to this affair that even Rees had not anticipated.

'That's right,' agreed Gail. 'I only got an acknowledgment card from him.'

'Did you know he shared an office with Alun?' asked North.

'No, he never mentioned it. I'm sure I would have remembered if he had told me. But there was no reason why he should have.'

So Rees had never mentioned that he shared an office with Carver. North wondered why. 'And what happened last Thursday night?'

'I only know what I've read in the papers: that Alun was run down outside St Stephen's entrance. And now it's being treated as murder, not an accident.'

'But you were expecting him to come here that night?' added North.

'Yes, but when he didn't turn up I wasn't surprised. You know what it's like. I just assumed it was another all-night sitting. I watched television and went to bed.'

'He didn't call, and you didn't call him?' There were so many telephones in the Commons, and the message service so reliable, that North wondered whether Rees had perhaps kept Gail at arm's length. He could understand why he might want to. She was a volatile, perhaps even unstable, mixture of vulnerability and determination.

'I never did. He was always very discreet ... he didn't want his wife to find out about us. You know she had once had him followed?'

'Are you sure?' North took marital infidelity somewhat for granted, and the thought of private detectives trailing errant husbands seemed rather old-fashioned ... as outdated as dirty weekends in Brighton.

'Alun was. He thought he recognised who it was ... one of his wife's boyfriends. There had been plenty, you know.'

'But if Alun was separated from his wife, why was he concerned about being followed?' North hesitated to delve into Rees's private life but he realised that the Speaker would be bound to cross-examine him about this part of the investigation later. It had to be done.

'He wanted access to the children. He didn't trust her and he was absolutely right not to. She is absolutely psychotic ... capable of *anything*, you know.' North raised his eyebrow at her emphasis. She continued undeterred. 'Alun wanted a legal agreement with Sheila and he didn't want our relationship to jeopardise that. I understood.'

'Were you planning a long-term relationship?' North ventured.

'Once Alun's solicitors had made a binding agreement with Sheila we were going to get married as soon as the decree absolute had come through.'

Or that's what he told her, thought North to himself. Could Rees have been sincere, or had he been stringing her along? 'Did you know Alun was on the point of becoming a wealthy man?' asked North casually, trying to avoid being caught studying her reaction.

Gail Crosby hesitated. 'I think that's rather private, don't you? It's not something I really want to talk about.'

North could see that he was now pushing the limits of her co-operation. 'I'm sure the police will mention it. Alun's inheritance might have a bearing on his death. Incidentally, why haven't you been to the police?' If she had really feared that Rees has been assassinated, North wondered why she had not seized the chance to ruin Roland Wells and expose the scandal she claimed to believe in.

'To say what?' Gail countered. 'I had no idea Alun had been murdered until I read about it in the papers. I had been weighing up whether to call them but in the end I decided that they'd probably come to me sooner or later. Why complicate matters? You found me soon enough. If the SAS man was really a professional, he will have covered his tracks by now.'

'I'm sure the police will want to see you,' North

said as he got up to leave. It was on this final point that she seemed almost disingenuous. She could have contacted the police as soon as she had read the papers. Why hadn't she done so? He didn't find her explanation at all convincing and realised this was an angle the police were better equipped to pursue. 'I think Sheila Rees had something to do with Alun's murder and anything you can tell them would be helpful. They're really working in the dark on this and the SAS man has to be caught.'

'Do you think Sheila Rees hired the SAS man to kill Alun?' asked Gail.

'It's a possibility,' admitted North, although he had not really given the proposition serious thought. 'It's something the police will want to pursue, I'm sure. Whoever murdered Alun will be caught, you can be certain of that.'

North made a note of Gail Crosby's telephone number and took his leave. He thought that if he stayed any longer she would turn all weepy on him. His task was to find Rees's killer, not comfort the bereaved. It was nearly four o'clock when he left the flat and he decided to walk back to the Commons. He needed the exercise and the stroll would give him an opportunity to think what he would tell Chief Inspector Young. North had no desire to drag Wells's name into the investigation just yet, but he knew he would have to disclose Gail's address. Some of what she had said certainly seemed to make sense. If Rees had checked up on his Northern Ireland source, that would have alerted the security authorities to his interest. No MP could expect to make inquiries about a member of a sensitive unit like the SAS, particularly in a Northern Ireland context, and not anticipate a reaction of just the kind that Vaughan had described: a call from the Chief Whip to find out what he was up to. If that was what had happened, the authorities would have a record of Rees's inquiry, and the name of the soldier.

North wondered where Mark Newman fitted into the picture. Was it a coincidence that he was directly connected with the PCW syndicate that Rees had been investigating? The police would have to see him, North thought . . . and his wife. Why had Elaine Newman omitted Rees's interest in City fraud from her list of his current parliamentary preoccupations?

North rehearsed what he was going to tell the police and drew up a list of those he would have to talk to again: Gwilym Williams to check on Gail's version of her meeting with Rees; Rhydian Vaughan in case the Opposition Chief Whip had come up with more on the security angle; and George Carver, Rees's room-mate, to see if he knew anything. However, the priority would be to find out the SAS man's identity. If he had had an appointment to see Rees sometime after the ten o'clock division, as Gail had claimed, he had become a definite murder suspect. SAS men were taught silent killing techniques as a matter of routine training, he reasoned, and pressure on the carotid artery was a classic method. That alone made him a candidate.

Once back at the Commons North walked into the Members' Lobby, and as he did so he was handed a pink slip by the doorkeeper manning the telephone message board. It was from Chief Inspector Young and it asked him to call Rochester Row urgently. North dialled the police station from one of the wall-mounted instruments.

'Chief Inspector, it's Philip North returning your call. I've some news for you—'

'There's been a major development,' Young cut in. 'We've traced the car that hit Rees and we've arrested the driver. It's Toby Bellington. You'd better let Mr Speaker know and come over right away if you can.'

North replaced the handset on to its cradle and paused for a moment. He had been so stunned by the news that Bellington had been arrested that he had neglected to say anything about Gail Crosby. Perhaps now there was no need, he thought, as he headed downstairs for a cab to the police station. As for the Speaker, he would have to wait.

At the police station North was shown up to the incident room by a uniformed constable and invited to wait in an interview room. Moments later Chief Inspector Young came in.

'Thanks for coming so quickly. What can you tell me about Bellington?' demanded the detective.

'He shares my office, for a start. I don't suppose he even knew Rees. His constituency is in Suffolk and he's been in the House for about twelve years. What more do you want to know?' North was uneasy about talking to the police about someone whom he counted as a personal friend. He had few enough in the Commons, and loyalty was important to him.

'Is he a heavy drinker?' continued Young, apparently oblivious to North's reluctance to inform on a friend.

'Yes, I suppose so. He lost his licence a while ago after being breathalysed, but he's got it back now. He used to have what you might term a drink problem.'

'Do you know where he was last Thursday night?'

'After he voted? I've no idea.'

'But not in your office?' pressed Young.

North wondered if he was taking the opportunity to establish North's movements too. It was not a topic North particularly wanted to discuss. 'He might have been,' said the MP casually. 'I certainly didn't see him, but I wasn't there. Is that where he says he was?'

'The trouble is, he says he can't remember where he was. But it was his car that hit Rees, there's no doubt.'

'How was it identified?' asked North, eager for all the details.

'One of the security people in the Commons carpark spotted a damaged Mercedes and reported it. It turns out to be Bellington's, and there are traces of blood on the front wing that match Rees's blood group. What I need from you is an insight into Bellington's motive.'

'So this was no accident?' queried North. How typical, he thought, of Bellington to have driven his car, uncleaned and unrepaired, into the Commons. What a bloody idiot.

'At this stage I have to assume that Bellington is directly involved and he knows the identity of an accomplice who was on the scene to finish off Rees after he had been run down.' Young's tone was neutral but North sensed his excitement.

'Bellington's a nice enough fellow ... I really can't imagine that he could be mixed up with a murder,' said North. 'He used to drink, he still gambles at a couple of Mayfair clubs, but he's no killer.'

'Doctor Crippen was a charmer too, and Hitler loved animals,' countered Young curtly. This was something he enjoyed saying to those who challenged him about suspects. 'Now, what did Bellington do before he came into the House?'

North accepted the admonition. 'He was a merchant banker in the City, and he still is. He's an Etonian ... went up to Christ Church I think, and his wife, an American incidentally, runs an art gallery in Notting Hill. A reasonable degree, and maybe even a short-service commission in the Army . . . I'm not sure. Toby's really very respectable . . . no skeletons in his cupboard. Two children, at Heathfield and Summerfield. The family lives in Eaton Terrace. His father was Colonial Secretary once upon a time.'

'You know a lot about him. What about his shoe size?' asked Young.

North ignored the sarcasm. 'Our office is pretty small. You get to know your colleagues when you share a tiny room with them for years at a time.'

'All eminently above board then?'

'In my opinion, very sound.' North was unsure whether the detective was mocking him.

'Did you know the Fraud Squad raided his bank ten days ago? And that one of his "clients" has been implicated in a money-laundering scheme in Gibraltar?'

'Chief Inspector.' North spoke slowly, with a trace of condescension. 'There's not a single person in the City who, at some stage in their career, hasn't rubbed shoulders with a scoundrel. MPs are no different, you know. Yet if an acquaintance turns out to be a wrong 'un it becomes headline news and a blurred photo of you both is dug out of some obscure picture library. If Toby was worried about some business deal that might explain his past problem with the bottle, but hundreds of people work for that bank and it is one of the most respected in the square mile. I can assure you he's not a crook . . . or even short of money as far as I know, and there's nothing to link him with Rees.'

'Apart from you,' said the detective softly. 'You share a room with Bellington and also happen to be Rees's pair. A coincidence?'

'Don't be absurd, Chief Inspector. Next you'll be saying that it's odd we're all MPs. Don't start trying to rope me in on this as well. You've got quite enough suspects at present anyway.'

'That's true enough,' murmured Young. 'If you would care to come next door I'll show you how many.' He led the way into the main incident room where two CID officers were working at desks, and a third uniformed officer in shirt-sleeves was talking on a telephone in the corner. At one end was a large blackboard with a represen-tation of the road outside St Stephen's entrance. A small rectangular box marked 'Rees' indicated where the man had fallen. Another box high-lighted with dotted lines showed where the police-man at the House of Lords had been on duty, and had moved to Rees. Two other boxes were attached by tape to the edge of the board where the names of individual witnesses were listed.

'As you can see, this is the murder scene,' explained Young. 'Here is Rees, and his assailant is close by. Three of those beside the body gave their names to the sergeant who had called the ambulance. So far we have two Japanese tourists and an MP.'

'That's not much, is it?' commented North. 'I thought quite a crowd gathered?'

'You have to add to that number the officer who caught a glimpse of the car. Thought it was a Mercedes, and he turns out to be right. His task was to find other witnesses who saw something ... not the inquisitive people who happened to drift by but didn't actually see the accident.'

'The murder,' corrected North.

'It was a road accident *then*,' Young pointed out. 'This only became a murder investigation on Saturday, as far as we are concerned, after the lab tests came through. And the public only became aware of that fact late last night.'

'So whoever strangled Rees probably thought they had got clean away with it until then.' North wandered over to the display and examined the taped sections. 'Will you eliminate the Japanese?'

'Probably. Special Branch have lent us their only Japanese-speaker and he is preparing their statements at the Park Lane Hotel. We'll check with the Tokyo police just to make sure they're not kung-fu experts who practise euthanasia, but I think we can probably rule them out at this stage.'

'And who are the blanks?'

'Two women. The first arrived at Rees's side very quickly. She had her back to the officer and was crouched over Rees and is a strong suspect. She had disappeared by the time the officer had returned from making his telephone call.'

'So Woman One could be almost anyone?'

'The officer had the impression that he had seen her around the Palace of Westminster before. Maybe an MP's wife or secretary. Quite young, a good-looker. He'd recognise her again. We'll call in Mrs Bellington on the off-chance.'

'Woman Two?' asked North.

'She seems to have replaced Woman One at the scene. Also a strong suspect. Was right beside the body for a few moments. The officer only glanced at her momentarily,' he added with obvious regret.

'And Roland Wells was the MP,' said North with surprise, reading from the blackboard.

'Know him? Not another of your office mates, I trust?' asked the detective.

'No, but he's a very able minister. Curiously enough his name cropped up in conversation this afternoon . . . with Rees's mistress.'

'So you've found her. That is good news. Where is she?'

'She lives in St George's Square and you certainly ought to interview her quickly. She came across to me as a bit flaky. From her accent I would guess that she is probably Canadian. Anyway, she's very upset and has some interesting theories, but you ought to hear them for yourself. Here's her telephone number. Her name is Gail Crosby.' North passed over a page from his notepad. 'She was Rees's research assistant.'

'On the payroll?'

'Modestly. It's not unusual. Lots of MPs sign up their wives as research assistants. Rees obviously preferred to employ his mistress. She was in quite a state and I didn't want to outstay my welcome.'

'So you were appropriately diplomatic?'

'Enough to establish that she hates Sheila Rees and was going to marry her husband.'

'So she wasn't a hooker?' asked Young.

North recoiled at his crudity. 'She wasn't in the rattlesnake league, like Sheila Rees. She's a nice, quiet, rather pathetic young creature who likes cats. And was mad about Rees.'

Young gave a low whistle. 'And where was she when this happened?' he asked, tapping the board.

'At home, waiting for Rees. He had moved in with her.'

'So his room at the NUR headquarters was really just for appearances. I thought as much. This is what they all do, is it?'

North caught what he thought might have been an accusation. 'If you are asking whether all MPs shack up with their staff, the answer is no,' North replied with a smile. 'But I admit the statistics are moving in your favour.'

'What did she have to say about Rees?'

'She'd only just heard his death was a murder so she was quite wound up. She knew that Rees had intended to meet someone late on the night he died, but she didn't know who.'

'There's a note in Rees's diary, the one recovered from his pocket, which refers to two possible appointments that evening.' Young paused. 'One says "S: 9.30"; the other is "TE: 10.30".'

'But no clue to the identity of either?' asked North.

'None,' said Young. 'The attendants in the Central Lobby have no recollection of anyone asking for Rees that night, but they have had to deal with literally hundreds of visitors during the past week. It's possible Rees did meet someone in the Central Lobby, or even in St Stephen's Hall, but if he did no one remembers it.'

'So what about Toby Bellington?' asked North, anxious at least to free his friend from suspicion of involvement in murder. 'How does he fit into all this?'

'I'm still not sure yet. He's downstairs in the cells and he'll be released once his solicitor has arrived and he's been charged.'

'What will the charge be? Not murder, surely?' pleaded North.

'That's an awkward one,' Young replied, stroking his chin. 'At the moment we can't charge him with anything except dangerous driving and failing to stop after an accident. We can't even bring causing death through dangerous or reckless driving because Rees died at the hands of whoever was with him after he had been hit by the car.'

'Have you told him that yet?'

'No, but his solicitor will realise there's something up when we don't go for the causing death charge under the Road Traffic Acts. The offences of dangerous driving and failing to stop are relatively minor. I will need evidence of a link between Bellington and the person on the pavement if a more serious charge is going to stick. When you think about it, your Mr Bellington has been remarkably lucky.'

'Why? I don't suppose he thinks so right now,' countered the MP.

'How many hit-and-run drivers leave a victim who promptly gets murdered?'

'Would Rees have died from the injuries he received when the car hit him?' In his mind North was already exploring possible lines of defence for Toby Bellington.

'That's a question for the inquest to decide. It will consider all the specialists' reports,' said the detective. 'Personally, I think Rees would have been very lucky to survive, but I'm no doctor. I'll take you down to see Bellington, and then I'll meet you here in the morning to interview Skelly, Rees's constituency agent. He may have an idea of who "S" and "TE" are in Rees's diary.'

'You're not assuming the "S" is Sheila Rees?' asked North, puzzled.

'Mr North, how could you think such a thing?' asked the detective with mock scorn. 'Surely you heard her yourself? She was at the cinema that evening, not at the Commons.'

'It was only a thought.' North smiled. 'I developed this unworthy idea that she might not have told the whole truth when I found out who the man was I'd recognised.'

'The childminder?' said Young.

'Actually Neil Roberts, once the Member for Alun Rees's seat. I just knew I'd seen him before somewhere,' said North, wishing he had made the connection earlier.

The MP followed Young out of the incident room and into the long corridor with the interview rooms. They went down two flights of concrete steps and across a large covered area that had a couple of patrol cars parked at one end, beside a black police van. Young led North up two short steps and then hammered on a solid steel door set into the brick wall. A Judas hole in the centre opened briefly, and then the door opened outwards.

'DCI Young,' the detective announced himself to the shirt-sleeved gaoler. 'This is Mr North who is helping me. I'd like to see Mr Bellington please.'

'Number three, sir,' replied the uniformed custody officer, glancing at his watch. 'The time is four fifty . . . DCI Young visiting three,' he called up the long bare corridor to someone who acknowledged out of sight. He then unlocked a heavy cell door and ushered North in. He was met by an overpowering stench of vomit, disinfectant and urine. Bellington, apparently unaffected by the powerful smell, was sitting on a long wooden ledge, his lanky legs folded under it. As North entered, Bellington got to his feet.

'It's all too ghastly, Philip,' he said unnecessarily. 'Can you imagine what the tabloids will make of this? I'm ruined. Can you imagine? I woke up this morning with hardly a care in the world, and now I'm facing a murder charge. God knows what Wendy will think.'

North exchanged glances with the detective. 'I'll leave you two gentlemen together, if you don't mind. When you want to leave, Mr North, just call the gaoler.'

'Thank you,' said North as Young banged the door shut behind him. He turned to Bellington. 'I don't think it's quite as bad as you might think, and you'll not be charged with murder today. But you must tell me what happened last Thursday.'

'I honestly don't know. We voted at ten, didn't we?'

'We were on two lines at ten, until the business was over. There was another division at around eleven. What did you do that day?'

Bellington buried his head in his hands. 'I spent the morning at the bank and had a lunch with British Telecom up their beastly tower. I was in the chamber for Defence Questions and I think I got called for a supplementary. Or was that on Wednesday? God, this is all a mess.'

'Go on,' urged North. 'After Questions where were you?'

'I had an hour or so with my secretary . . . not in the office but on the committee corridor . . . and then I had a meeting of the East Anglia Members Committee. I gave a couple of farmers a drink in the Pugin Room at six, and then I had one with that old soak from the *Mail* in Annie's.'

'Where was dinner?' pressed North.

'A training board do in Dining-Room B or was it C? One of the smaller ones.'

'And lots to drink there too?' North wondered why he had put the question. It was not an unusual list of engagements, but it took a heavy toll on a man's liver. No one could get away from Annie's, the bar particularly favoured by the lobby journalists, without downing at least two stiff ones. There would also have been refreshments served in the private dining-room before dinner.

'About average, I think,' replied Bellington, unoffended. 'I remember voting at ten, and then I knew I was paired for the rest of the evening. I don't remember getting my car up from the garage, but I suppose I must have done. I may have met someone, I suppose.'

'So after the ten o'clock division you had a few drinks then left the House?'

'I'm pretty sure I did,' nodded Bellington wretchedly. 'God knows how I got home . . . I must have been pretty far gone.'

'When you drive home, what route do you usually take?'

'Victoria Street . . . but if I've had a few I cut through Pimlico . . . saves driving past Scotland Yard or through the speed traps on the river. Fat lot of good that's done me now.'

'So there is a good chance that you did leave Parliament Square, heading west along the Embankment at about eleven?'

'I suppose so. It's awfully good of you to try and help, Philip, but I suppose I must have run the bugger down. The police seem convinced.' He paused for a moment as another thought dawned on him. 'Christ, Rees was your pair, wasn't he? I am sorry, Philip.' It was almost as if the inconvenience North would suffer was more significant than the Welshman's death.

'You may have hit Rees,' said North, ignoring Bellington's lack of remorse, 'but you didn't kill him. I think I'm getting close to the truth, but proving it will be rather more difficult.'

Chapter Six

The Agent

Paul Skelly was a political animal of a quite different kind to North. That much was clear within moments of his interview starting at Rochester Row police station early on Thursday morning. He had been hostile from the beginning when DCI Young had introduced the rather younger Tory MP as Rees's friend and a procedural advisor to the police on the inquiry. Skelly only accepted his presence – with marked reluctance – when he had been assured that his candour would not be used for party political advantage.

'Our internal wrangles are healthy,' protested Skelly in a rich Welsh accent. 'They may not appear so to the outsider, but at least we are indulging in genuine debate. Not even the most ardent Tory would bother to pretend that their conference is anything more than a sham. Yes, we talk out our policies. I make no apology for that. But it's an authentic process. Who knows how Tory Party manifestos are conjured up? We may leave some blood on the carpet, metaphorically speaking, but once the agenda has been exhausted we know we have reached a policy decision fairly and democratically, after everyone has had their say. That's the crucial difference.

'Alun had every opportunity of doing well,' he continued. 'He arrived unencumbered, without the labels that sometimes handicap new Members.'

Whilst North could not have agreed with much of what Skelly had said, he did recognise the validity of this particular observation. Just as Tory businessmen, however successful, never managed to come to terms with the mauling they received on the floor of the House, and usually made poor ministers, their Labour counterparts fared equally badly. Those who came to the Commons with reputations already established in the unions or even the academic world never made the necessary adjustment to the rough and tumble of debate in the chamber. Rees had been largely unknown before his election and this had held him in good stead amongst his new, ever-critical colleagues.

'He was popular in the constituency and I dare say he would have been offered promotion given enough time,' Skelly claimed, somewhat unconvincingly.

North had done his homework on the man and knew what to expect. Skelly was fifty-four years old, and had spent his life in the Labour movement, graduating from what had then been the

Young Communist League into the left of main-
stream socialism. It was a paradox of recent political history that in the past months he had been
obliged to satisfy the national headquarters in
Walworth Road that none of his branches had
been penetrated by Militant, Vanguard, Socialist
Challenge or Class War. The irony lay in the fact
that these groups, now designated extremist and
proscribed, had maintained a commitment to
Clause Four and other policies, now branded vote-
losers, that had been the platform for the great
victories of 1945 and 1964.

Skelly was a paid party activist, and he was
wholly absorbed by the party. He had little life
outside the Labour ranks, and whatever spare
time he had was devoted to furthering the party,
either by canvassing for new members or drum-
ming up more support from the comparatively
apathetic Labour clubs in the constituency. His
commitment was total and North was aware that
he cared little what impression he made on this
particular audience: a Tory politician and two
senior police officers, one of whom he was convinced was working for Special Branch.

This was not to say that Skelly raised any
objections when asked to judge the ideological
credentials of his comrades. This was a necessary
step to achieving power and, given the current
climate of political opinion, a degree of trimming
was required. Nevertheless, when gently pro-
voked by Young's skilled interrogation, Skelly

recalled wryly how he had been appalled by Harold Wilson's 'expediency'. His compromises, he asserted, looked tame in comparison with the somersaults that had been performed since the last disastrous election results.

Of course, North knew that terms like 'disastrous' were relative in a Welsh context. The Labour Party had dominated the scene for years, leaving Plaid Cymru and the Liberals to an insignificant Celtic fringe. Cardiff had prospered under Labour and had much to fear from the Nationalists who were concentrated in the rural north of the principality. Even the benefits of steel and coal privatisation had done nothing to dampen the strong traditional support for Labour in the valleys of south Wales. Members like Alun Rees had been assured of re-election at the polls. The only hurdle for them was reselection by the local party.

'That was where Neil Roberts had come unstuck,' explained Skelly. Roberts – Rees's predecessor – had been unseated after a bitter struggle on the General Management Committee. One group on the left had campaigned vigorously against Roberts's readoption, claiming that his voting record in the Commons against measures specifically endorsed by conference had demonstrated an intellectual arrogance that was the hallmark of closet Tories, the so-called centre-right of the party. Roberts, who had admittedly neglected the rank and file membership, had been isolated with few friends among the old-timers who might have backed Roberts despite his Bloomsbury pretensions, but even they recognised the validity of the accusations 'Bollinger Bolshevik' and 'armchair socialist'. There had also been one too many references to Roberts, the Welsh Lothario, by gossip columnists attending the fashionable dinner parties in Tite Street and Vincent Square to gain him the friends he really needed in the smoke-filled snooker halls behind the Labour clubs where the loyalties that carried weight were won and lost.

Skelly was not entirely at ease when he described how Roberts, aged only fifty-one, had been supplanted by an improbable coalition of the hard left, determined to be rid of Roberts, and the old guard who were keen to ally themselves with someone who represented the technological future. Rees had been the compromise candidate, acceptable to both wings who had initially fought hard for their own men. This was the kind of internal linen-washing exercise that was best kept behind closed doors, not recounted in front of two uncomprehending London policemen, and certainly not for the ears of a Tory, whatever his status in a murder investigation.

'Was there any lingering bitterness on the part of the candidates he defeated for selection?' asked Young.

'Neil Roberts never anticipated the challenge, but he held no personal grudge against Alun.

As I've already explained, there were two other contenders for the seat. Alun was almost an afterthought. If Neil had any scores to settle, they would have been with the two original challengers.'

'But Rees did take Roberts's job, in effect,' observed Shawcross.

'That's true,' agreed Skelly, 'and Neil wasn't happy about any of it, but he would never have resorted to violence. I knew him as well as anyone, and he isn't that sort of man.'

'You were his agent too?' queried Young.

'I'm the constituency agent for the party, whoever is the Member. My loyalty is, first and foremost, to the party. But, yes, I looked after them both.'

'Did you know of any enemies who might have wanted to harm Rees?' asked the detective.

'I've given this a lot of thought since you first contacted me,' said Skelly carefully. 'It was quite a shock to learn that Alun had been murdered. There are two possibilities in my view. He had done a lot to antagonise Meibion Glyndwr, the so-called Sons of Owen Glendower . . . you know, very outspoken, condemning them at every opportunity. We had heard "the boys" were out to get him.'

'A specific threat?' asked Young.

'Not exactly, but these people are fanatics. You have to take them seriously, even if they're still stuck in the fifteenth century.'

'Who are they?' asked North, intrigued.

'Fascists, really,' he answered contemptuously. 'They've manufactured a historical myth about Owen Glendower, but none of it stands up to examination. Glendower formed the first parliament in Wales all right, but it only lasted eighteen months. When he was defeated by the English he was fighting other Welshmen too. The Nationalists prefer to overlook that. This modern Meibion Glyndwr is utterly fraudulent ... a middle-class terrorist group spawned in the universities.'

'So they're a sort of Baader-Meinhof gang ... well off and well educated but not much common sense?' suggested the MP.

'They're very few of them active, and they all got mixed up in the colleges.'

'I'm advised that there aren't many left, apart from a few among the language fanatics in the north. Is that right?' asked Young.

'There's probably a hard core of twenty altogether, spread across the principality, but they're dangerous. Some of them have military backgrounds. You hear rumours in the pubs and clubs about who has the right connections. We hear the chat and word gets around. It may all be bar talk, but they're not worth messing with. However, that didn't deter Alun. He labelled them as terrorists who hadn't the courage to face defeat in the ballot-box and that seemed to hit home. He was an irritant to them though I never really believed it would come to this – running him down in a London street.'

'You haven't read about Rees in the papers?' asked Young.

'Not yet. With Rees dead, I've been too busy these last few days on constituency matters. What do you mean?'

'Rees wasn't killed by a hit-and-run driver. In fact a Member of Parliament was charged yesterday evening with dangerous driving, but we are still pursuing a murder inquiry. It involves a bomb, and it would appear to be a terrorist incident. I can say little more at this stage,' Young added with characteristic caution.

'The Sons of Owen Glendower have a long history of bomb-making, not all of it very successful.' Skelly was referring to the investiture of the Prince of Wales, which had been marred by the deaths of two extremists in Caernarfon who had been blown up while preparing their own device.

'You mentioned two possible enemies. Who is the second?' asked Young.

'Alun had also campaigned against the Freemasons and there had been a lot of bad feeling locally on the subject, particularly on the council. Not all masons are corrupt, mind you, as Alun sometimes tended to imply. He had been threatened with a libel action after some choice words in the *Evening Herald* and he was none too popular in the lodges.'

'What had prompted that?'

'We had a scandal on the planning committee a couple of years ago. A developer was granted permission to build an industrial park in what was really green belt. Someone tipped off the paper that some of the councillors who had voted the application through were connected to the builder. They were all members of the same lodge. After that, Alun agreed to sponsor a Private Members' Bill requiring all Freemasons serving on local authorities to declare their membership. It unleashed a tremendous furore, right across the country.'

'But especially in the constituency?' Young asked. He remembered some of his own colleagues looking a little green about the gills when it had been suggested that all senior police officers should be obliged to declare their membership of the brotherhood.

'Well, some saw it as a form of discrimination. I didn't, mind, but we never really knew who was, and who wasn't.'

'A mason?'

'Yes. Alun could never really be sure of his own supporters. We didn't know who the masons were. We suspected, of course, but didn't really know. I had warned Alun when the whole thing started. "Be sure of your ground here," I'd said. There's no telling where these people are. They don't publicise their involvement. I think in retrospect Alun realised he had taken on too much. He ought to have done more research to find out exactly who the opposition was.'

'But if he was threatened with a libel action, he must have known the source?'

'Not really. The solicitor's letter apparently was sent on the instructions of the entire lodge. No single individual complainant was identified.'

'Do you have that correspondence?'

'Oh, no. Alun looked after all his own letters. Gwen in the office only did party work. Everything else went to his snooty secretary at the Commons.'

Young appeared to ignore the remark. 'Were there any other controversies, of a purely local nature, that might have provided someone with an excuse?'

'A couple of the union branches were unhappy about the prospect of losing jobs at the recycling plant, but you couldn't really say that was a motive for murder. Anyway, most of the constituency backed Alun on that. The place is a disgrace and it's been poisoning the district for years.'

'And what about the management? How did they feel about Rees stirring up trouble?'

'They had a confrontation two weeks ago after Alun had gone on local television to highlight the problem. The managing director said all the processes were perfectly safe so Alun challenged him to drink a flask of liquid that supposedly had been collected from an outfall into a neighbouring stream. The director had stormed off the set. It was only afterwards that Alun had admitted that the liquid was nothing more dangerous than tap-water. Word got back to the company and they were furious. Of course, they'd been made to look complete idiots by Alun. It was a tremendous coup.'

'But didn't win him many friends?' asked Young as he made a note to get a videocassette of the television broadcast.

'I suppose not,' acknowledged the agent, 'but it demonstrated that the company didn't really have any confidence in its own claims.'

'So in order of preference,' concluded the police officer, 'you would identify the potential political assassins as the Sons of Owen Glendower, the Freemasons and the chemical company?'

'When you put it like that I suppose the Sons of Owen Glendower are the most probable.'

'And surely the masons can be eliminated,' said North. 'They're harmless enough.'

'Yes,' said Young. 'But don't forget there was a masonic angle to the murder of that Italian banker who was found hanged under Blackfriars Bridge in London a few years ago. And I wouldn't necessarily exclude a renegade who had been up to mischief and feared that his corrupt behaviour was in danger of being exposed by Rees. That wouldn't require a masonic conspiracy; merely a vulnerable member of a lodge. I'll keep an open mind on that.' Young then turned again to Skelly. 'I understand that Rees stayed with you when he went down to his constituency. What can you tell me about his domestic arrangements?'

'He had left his wife and they were going to get a divorce.'

'He left her, or she left him?' interrupted Young.

'Let's just say they parted.'

'This is important,' pressed the detective. 'You must be entirely candid with me over this matter. I know that Rees had moved in with a girlfriend in London and I have grounds to believe that his relationship with his estranged wife may be a significant factor in his murder.'

The agent looked rather taken aback. 'I don't know anything about his life in London. I rarely come up here and MPs keep their parliamentary life quite separate from their constituency business. I don't know anything about a girlfriend . . . nor do I want to know anything. That's not relevant – for me or the party.'

'So it's a surprise to you that Rees had acquired a girlfriend in London?' demanded Young.

'It's news to me but he wouldn't tell me anyway. Why should he?'

'Didn't you have to know where to reach him at any time?'

'If there was ever anything urgent I would telephone him at the Commons. He always called back very quickly. He was very efficient about returning his messages.'

'And what were your relations like with Mrs Rees?'

'I had no time for her, and she had no interest in the party. She didn't go to conference or attend branch meetings. She was trouble, and I'm not alone in thinking that.'

'Then she was less than an ideal parliamentary wife?'

'I don't know if there is such a thing, but she was no good in the constituency. Always making trouble. Always flirting. She was an embarrassment to Alun and I was pleased when they split up. Of course, it's sad for the children, but that can't be helped.'

'Was she having an affair at the time of Rees's murder?'

'I really couldn't say. We've had nothing to do with her since they went their separate ways and we never talked about her in the house. No reason to.'

'But what about in the past?' Young wasn't going to let Skelly off the hook just yet. 'Isn't it true that she had an affair with Neil Roberts?'

Skelly hesitated, and looked uncertain for a moment. 'I don't know who's been telling you what, but I can't see how gossip can be of any relevance to your investigation.'

'Permit me, Mr Skelly, to be the best judge of that,' Young replied icily. 'Alun Rees was murdered. My job is to find the murderer and to do so I need to know everything about Rees's life. You have my assurance that whatever you tell me will go no further if it turns out to be irrelevant to the matter in hand. Detective Inspector Shawcross attended the funeral yesterday and has also spoken to the local police. If we are to solve this crime we need your co-operation. So, once again, what can you tell me about Sheila Rees and Neil Roberts?'

'They had an affair, it's true. It was very public knowledge. It was also very humiliating for Alun, taking everything into consideration.'

'You mean the fact that Roberts had been the MP?'

'It was almost, well, *incestuous*, if you know what I mean. How could she have done it? It was really terrible for Alun.'

'How did it happen?'

'It was all rumour, you know. Never anything definite, but it was always said that Roberts's car was parked outside the Rees's house in the afternoon. You can imagine the stories, I expect. And knowing Sheila, we were inclined to believe them. Alun certainly did.'

'Did he ever confront Roberts?'

'As far as I know they never saw each other. Alun never told me if he did.'

'And what did Roberts do after the general election?'

'He got a job with the Welsh Industrial Development Agency. Very high-powered, bringing new business to the area, and didn't do him any harm politically either. He has an office in Cardiff and spends a lot of time in London as well.'

'And did he continue to see Sheila Rees?' asked Young.

'You'd have to ask her that,' said Skelly uneasily.

'I'm asking you,' insisted the detective.

'I think so, yes,' replied the agent with much reluctance.

'I see. And what about Mrs Roberts?'

'Rhona is in a psychiatric hospital, and I don't suppose she'll ever come out. She's been there for years.'

'Do you know which one?' interrupted Shawcross.

'If she hasn't been moved, it's St Lythan's, out towards Barry.'

'And one final formality, Mr Skelly ... Can you tell me where you were on the night of the murder?'

'I was over in Llanedeyrn, interviewing a possible councillor. We have a by-election pending in that ward and I was attending a branch meeting at the Labour club. Afterwards we had a few drinks, and then I went home.'

'Are you going back to Wales now?'

'I have another meeting this afternoon, and then I'll catch the last train tonight. But I have a question for you. How did Alun die? I thought he'd been hit by a car, and you said it was murder, and now you tell me that an MP has been charged with dangerous driving, but there's a bomb involved? It doesn't make sense. How *did* he die?'

'Suffice to say that his murderer is still at liberty and we have several lines of inquiry to pursue before we can make any public comment. Your help has been invaluable.'

Skelly recognised that he had been dismissed. He left the room, looking puzzled, and Shawcross escorted him to the entrance.

In Shawcross's temporary absence Young and North went through the accumulated evidence together. 'I assume from the thrust of your questions to Skelly that Roberts is now a strong suspect.' North was keen to clarify the relevance of Skelly's testimony.

'Yes. And you were quite right when you said you thought you recognised Neil Roberts as the man who answered the door when we went to interview Sheila Rees on Tuesday evening. It seems he was rather more than a convenient baby-sitter. However, if he had conspired with her I would not have expected to see him there. Our appointment had been made ahead of time and if they had wanted to conceal their relationship it would have been simpler for him to have remained in the background.'

'So is this a domestic murder or a political assassination?'

'I think the political aspect is reasonably straightforward. Rees was a prestige target and the Welsh extremists may have decided to go for him. Then we have the domestic element which, coincidentally, meant that someone was out to poison him at much the same time.'

'If we can take the political aspect first; why Rees?' North asked. 'He was hardly what you term a prestige target. There are six hundred and forty-nine MPs, and of that number there are probably three hundred who have almost no national profile at all and are only known to their own constituents. Indeed, some are not known even to them.'

'Rees may have had a face that fitted, if that is the right phrase,' said Young. 'All the high-risk politicians now have pretty good security, thanks to the Provisionals. Terrorists know that things have really been tightened up in recent years, and that there is a definite chance that they will be detected if they go for a big name. But, as you rightly say, Rees wasn't in that category . . . he wasn't a household name. But his hostility to the Sons of Glendower must have been an irritant to them, and that might have been enough to give him stature, at least within their own circle. He made himself a target, if you catch my drift. And there's another thing. To the public, all MPs enjoy a certain cachet. Getting close enough to someone of rank to plant a bomb in his car is in itself something of a coup. The terrorist's principal objectives are publicity and overreaction. The media has a field day however obscure the politician and this achieves what the terrorist wants. No, Rees was a good target for the Sons of Glendower. Special Branch have assigned one of their men to the case and he'll liaise with the Welsh end. They're convinced this is an authentic case of terrorism.'

'So how many murderers are you after? The Sons of Glendower, the poisoner . . . and who else?'

'Special Branch will handle the terrorist angle. The forensic scientists at Fort Halstead have compiled a detailed report on the device and it's up to the Glamorgan police, working with our Branch, to sift through their list of likely suspects to find the bomber. All these extremist groups are well penetrated by the Branch and the Security Service, and there are only a limited number of activists who possess the right knowledge to build a viable bomb. It's not as easy as the newspapers would have you believe and the clumsy ones don't last long. Those who survive are known to us. That leaves the poisoner. A domestic crime, and usually perpetrated by females.'

'Sheila Ross?'

'She had the motive, with her husband getting a windfall, and she obviously resented his involvement with other women in London, or so she said, but there's a question mark over opportunity. Even if she was the "S" in Rees's diary, and had a meeting with him that evening, how could she administer the poison unless she was seeing him regularly? The lab says a substantial quantity had built up in the vital organs.'

'But there aren't too many other suspects.'

'There's the mistress, Gail Crosby. I'm interviewing her later today.'

'She had the opportunity to poison Alun,' North agreed, 'but hardly the motive. He had left his wife for her, and they would be sharing a fortune. Judging by the state of her flat, she could do with the money.'

'Which is now going to Sheila Rees,' said Young thoughtfully. 'But then we also have Mrs Roberts. The Glamorgan police are going to have to check that she was still in hospital at the time of the incident.'

'Which leaves us with Rees's secretary,' said North. 'She had plenty of opportunity, but no obvious motive. I've been through as much of his correspondence as there is, but there's no hint that their relationship wasn't anything more than she says it was. Frigid, in a word.'

'I'm seeing her this afternoon. She seems to have put Skelly's back up. I wonder why? Did you ask her where she was at the time of the murder?'

'It never occurred to me that she might be a suspect,' North declared apologetically. 'And what about the strangler? How does that person fit in with the terrorist and the poisoner?'

'There we have the real puzzler,' admitted the detective. 'How did whoever finished off Rees know he'd be just there? It implies collusion between your friend, Toby Bellington, and whoever was on hand to administer the coup de grâce. From a scientific standpoint, there are only two possible explanations. Either someone was stalking Rees, and he or she simply took the opportunity when it presented itself so fortuitously, or there was an elaborate scheme to entrap Rees at the moment he emerged from St Stephen's entrance. The latter scenario seems improbable, given that the forensic evidence links Bellington to the offending vehicle, and it would seem from his statement that his behaviour was entirely unpredictable. He might easily have taken a different route home and there was no certainty that he would run down Rees. No, we have to go for the more difficult option: someone was on hand to kill Rees when the chance arose.'

'But that's an extraordinary coincidence, isn't it?' said North. 'That someone happened to be there to kill Rees. Why there? Why then?'

'The textbooks say policemen don't believe in coincidences, but this one does,' said Young. 'It may just be that someone was out to kill an MP, any MP, and he or she recognised Rees. However, I realise that's a long shot. We really need to identify every person on the scene.'

'At present you have the minister, two unidentified women and two Japanese tourists. Any leads?'

'I have an appointment with Roland Wells at four, in his office in the Commons, so perhaps you could sit in on it.'

'I'd be pleased to, Chief Inspector,' said North, as Inspector Shawcross re-entered the room.

'I will have spoken to the Crosby woman by then, so perhaps we can compare notes. Can we meet in the Central Lobby at ten to?'

'But before we go . . . any news from the funeral?' North looked at Shawcross.

'Only that Sheila Rees and Neil Roberts have been conducting an affair continuously since they met . . . and the talk was that when Roberts was a lad he used to be a Welsh Nationalist. Quite a little firebrand in his day, so the story goes.'

Young and North exchanged glances. It looked as though Roberts was long overdue for an interview. And so was his lover.

Chapter Seven

The Minister

North need not have worried about the detectives' reaction to Gail Crosby's revelations. In fact, when they met, there was no time to discuss her testimony because the two detectives, both tight-lipped, had been held up by the queue for the security search at St Stephen's entrance. Despite their warrant cards, they had been made to submit to the complete search, and they were a few minutes late when they hurried into the Central Lobby to meet North. The MP had been eager to hear what had transpired with Rees's mistress, but neither man was willing to be drawn.

'Whether you realised it or not, sir,' opened Young when he was introduced to Roland Wells, 'you were a witness to a murder and your memory of exactly what happened that night is the best lead we have to solving this crime.'

North, Shawcross and the Detective Chief Inspector were in Roland Wells's office in the Commons, a small panelled room in the ministerial corridor almost directly under the chamber.

North had waited impatiently for the two police
officers in Central Lobby and had guided them
across the Members' Lobby and into the stairwell
beside the Members' Post Office. From the Members' Lobby he had taken them through the labyrinth of narrow passageways and across one of
the Palace of Westminster's innumerable courtyards to reach what most Members regarded as
the inner sanctum of power, the complex of rooms
in which government authority was concentrated.
Each minister, however junior his rank, was allocated a room here so he or she could conduct their
parliamentary business as well as attend to their
departmental responsibilities. Parliamentary
under-secretaries, the lowest in the ministerial
pecking order, were granted a mere cubby-hole.
A minister of state received rather larger accommodation, while a secretary of state usually
achieved an office big enough to entertain up to
a dozen rebels at a time. That, North explained,
was one of the functions of the minister's Parliamentary Private Secretary who met them outside
Roland Wells's door and had made the introductions. The PPS was the invaluable link between
the backbenchers and the minister, the departmental bottle-washer who sniffed out trouble
among the troops and gave them opportunities to
air grievances over a glass of warm white wine
in the privacy of the ministerial room, rather
than in *Hansard*.

Wells's PPS was David Grant, an ambitious

young solicitor who was clinging to a very slight majority in Nottingham. North knew Grant's reputation as a very assiduous PPS, distributing the yellow Parliamentary Question forms to his more compliant colleagues in good time for Questions. Each had been prefilled with a question to which the department had already prepared a comprehensive answer, and all were favourable to the government. Grant thought up the individual questions, ensured that his minister's private office retained a copy, and then persuaded accommodating backbenchers to put their names to them. The objective was to fill the order paper with planted topics so that a high proportion would be among the dozen or so selected for oral answer in the chamber during Questions. The procedure allowed the minister to look good in the House, especially to the wider public which would be impressed by his grasp of his brief. For the cognoscenti, the minister's performance on his feet actually reflected more on his PPS, crouching low on the bench directly behind him, ready to take advice from the officials in the box beside the Speaker's Chair if an unexpected issue was raised, than on the minister himself.

Grant's career as PPS was not an untypical gamble. If promoted to a ministerial post in the next reshuffle, as had been widely tipped by the sephologists, he would be obliged to give up his partnership, as required under the rules governing ministers' outside business interests. But this would place him at a disadvantage in relation to his other partners if, as he anticipated, he lost his seat at the next election and had to return to his practice while he sought a new, and preferably safer, seat. His dilemma was whether to decline office in this parliament and retain his lucrative legal income which helped pay for the education of his two children, knowing that there was a risk he might never get another chance at a department, or whether he ought to leap at the opportunity for advancement and rely on the bank to tide him over the financial consequences. North didn't envy him his dilemma.

This particular interview was outside Grant's area of responsibility so once he had shown the three visitors into the minister's office he had left discreetly and waited outside ready to intercept possible interruptions. He had agreed with North to escort the two policemen back to the Central Lobby once the meeting was over, leaving North with Wells to propose a change in the export credit guarantee system, a subject that North had suddenly developed an interest in so as to obtain a few minutes with Wells on his own. This, at least, had been his explanation to the two detectives and to the PPS, but in reality his concern was Gail Crosby's story of blackmail and intrigue. He had not confided in Young, mindful of Mr Speaker's views on the preservation of parliamentary reputations, but the allegations were too serious to be ignored.

North had spent a restless night wondering what action he should take. If Wells was being blackmailed he might, he reasoned, welcome an opportunity to share the burden with a sympathetic colleague who presented no threat. Such matters could hardly be discussed with the Chief Whip or other cabinet colleagues without the Prime Minister's instant intervention. That would most likely spell the end of a promising career that should be destined for a cabinet portfolio. Certainly Wells was ambitious enough to rise to high office. He was known to enjoy the rather meagre trappings of ministerial power now in his grasp, the Austin Allegro with a notoriously insecure cellular telephone, the black Glaswegian driver from the Government Car Service and the red dispatch boxes. He coveted the private initiation ceremony at which a newly appointed secretary of state received his seals of office from the monarch, kissed hands, and was admitted to the Privy Council once the secret oath had been administered; the impressive medallion, held by his driver, that would give him the right to drive across the royal parks and through the convenient short cut of Horseguards Parade; and the secret instruction on how to communicate directly to the sovereign, by-passing the palace staff, by putting his initials on a particular corner of the envelope. Such were the intangible assets of a cabinet minister that represented the pinnacle of political power in Britain.

North recognised there were very real risks
involved in meddling in such a sensitive issue at
such an elevated level. Disgrace would inevitably
follow any public hint of misconduct, and the
unpalatable fact was that Wells was vulnerable
even if the allegations were untrue. There had
been countless cases of unfounded rumour in the
Commons developing sufficient momentum to
threaten the most innocent and unlikely of
people. Unfortunately almost everyone, at one
time or another, had said or done something that
could be open to misinterpretation. Perhaps it
was something as trivial as a joke in poor taste,
or an unguarded remark to a journalist. For
others, with an authentic skeleton in the cupboard, progress up the ladder of promotion meant
a greater height from which to fall, and an
increased burden of guilt. If it involved an illegit-
imate child, perhaps the result of a youthful
indiscretion, or the embarrassment of a liaison
with a hooker, the unexploded bomb could be det-
onated at any time by one of the Sunday tabloids.
Mere infidelity could probably be survived, but
a wholly legal act of homosexuality would spell
catastrophe for the upwardly mobile. Banana
skins littered the political scene ready to unseat
the unwary.

Such matters were not, of course, raised by the
two detectives who were anxious to identify every
person who had rushed to Rees's aid after he had
been hit by the Mercedes. Wells had been on his

way to a television interview on College Green. He had been allocated a live slot just after the last division and had been on his way to fulfil the engagement when the accident had occurred. Once Young had explained what had really happened, after cautioning the minister to secrecy over the exact cause of Rees's death, Wells had described each of the other people he had noticed at the scene. A few tourists, including the Japanese pair, two or maybe three women, perhaps an older woman, and the couple to whom he had been speaking just before the incident. Wells supplied the last two names to Inspector Shawcross who made a note of them in his pad.

The minister remained seated behind his large desk and rested his chin on his fists. He was in his late fifties, and was popular with his colleagues. Wells had removed his half-moon spectacles and his eyes studied the three members of his audience. To North he appeared perfectly composed. No sign of the pressure a blackmailer would have put him under, no indication of any of the stereotypical behaviour associated with flustered, closet homosexuals faced with imminent exposure and inevitable disgrace.

'I didn't really see the, er, collision myself, you understand. I heard the awful thud and looked over. There was a crumpled figure on the ground, with people running to help. I stood to one side because I have no first-aid training and there were other more competent people about. What should one do? In my day one wasn't supposed to move someone who had been injured in case of a broken rib puncturing the lung or heart, but that's all changed now, hasn't it?' It was a rhetorical question. 'I seem to remember reading that there's more danger now from people choking and the priority is to make sure the windpipe is clear. One of the women looked very competent . . . seemed to take charge while the policeman went to telephone for an ambulance. She gave me the impression she knew what she was doing. I didn't want to interfere. Terrible business. I gather that in New York nobody will help in these situations . . . afraid they'll be sued later. I once heard that even doctors will cross the street to avoid giving a helping hand and being thanked with a medical malpractice suit afterwards.'

'Can you describe the first woman on the scene?' asked Shawcross, setting a businesslike tone.

'Youngish, quite good looking . . . exuded confidence if you know what I mean. Short hair, dark I think.'

'How old? Twenty, thirty?' interrupted the DCI, having abandoned his slightly deferential attitude.

'Thirties, I suppose. The light wasn't particularly good and I really wasn't concentrating on her. It was poor old Rees. Quite a shock when I realised who it was.'

'Did you touch him?' Young asked the question

quietly, but North noticed how Shawcross was concentrating on his notebook, ready to record the minister's answer.

'I don't think so,' replied Wells, apparently oblivious to the significance of the question. 'I knelt down beside him for a moment . . . instinctive I suppose, but then I stepped back. Not much really I could do.'

'Would you recognise either of the women there if you saw them again?'

'Probably. There was another chap who was behaving rather oddly . . . a bit unsteady on his feet . . . smartly dressed young man.'

'How close did he get to Rees?'

'I'm not sure. He was not exactly with one of the women . . . but they definitely knew each other. In fact I think they went off together when the police officer started to take names.'

'Anyone else there you noticed?'

'Another man caught my eye . . . thickset type, in jeans. He was there one moment and gone the next. You know how it is. A crowd gathers, all the faces are a blur because of the shock.'

'So there were at least five people close to Rees, excluding yourself.'

'That's right. It's rather a sobering thought that I might have witnessed a murder without even realising it. Why would anyone do such a thing? Rees was a pain in the neck, but hardly a national figure.'

'There is certainly a terrorist involvement in

this, but as yet we have reached no firm con-
clusions,' said Young ambiguously. 'Can you tell
me what your movements were earlier in the
evening?'

'I was in my office at the DTI,' said Wells, referring to his diary, 'in Victoria Street, until about
seven, and then I was driven to the Commons for
a reception in the CPA rooms ... a Common-
wealth parliamentary delegation. I did a radio
interview for one of the radio news programmes
in the Bridge Street studios at seven fifty, and
then I had a dinner to speak at.'

'In the House?'

'Yes, one of the dining-rooms downstairs. It was
the East Midlands CBI, organised by a colleague.
I spoke until the division, and then I went to vote.
Then I was scheduled to do a live interview on
College Green.'

'Finally, Minister, a few formalities. How well
did you know Rees?'

'Hardly at all. He had never come to see me in
my ministerial capacity although he had tabled
quite a few questions for the department. You
might like to get the details from my PPS. He
monitors the awkward squad on the Opposition
benches.'

'There was no personal animosity between
you?'

'None. But now you come to mention it, I did
see his predecessor that evening.'

'And who was that, sir?' asked Young blandly.

Wells turned to North for a moment. 'Didn't Neil Roberts have Rees's Cardiff seat before the last election?'

North nodded in confirmation but it was Young who pursued the matter. 'You saw Neil Roberts in the Commons that Thursday night?'

'I'm pretty sure I did,' said Wells, with a trace of uncertainty in his voice. 'I think he was in the library corridor when we went through for the division. That's right. I nodded to him as a familiar face . . . and I only realised a few moments later that he was no longer a Member.'

'Is that usual?'

'Oh, yes. Ex-Members are allowed into the Members' Lobby and you often see them there after dinner. They've usually been dining in the House and it's the best place to spot old friends. We have a regular dinner, the Dinosaurs, and I suppose the other side do much the same for their ex-Members. Yes, it was Neil Roberts all right. Clever fellow . . . good on his feet as I recall. More than a match for Rees I would have thought, but who can tell what goes on in the Labour Party?'

'Are you sure you saw him in the library corridor, and not outside?'

'I certainly didn't see him near Rees, if that's what you mean. I would certainly have remembered that. But he was definitely in the Commons when the division was called. I'd swear it was him.'

'You may have to, sir,' answered Young. 'And

one final point. I'm sorry to ask, but it's just routine. Are you a Freemason by any chance?'

'I can't really see that it has anything to do with your investigation but, as it happens, I am.' Wells's voice had undergone a distinct change in tone. This question had been decidedly unwelcome.

The two policemen excused themselves, but North stayed behind as Grant steered them from the room. Once alone, Wells exploded with indignation.

'The bloody impudence. Asking a minister of the Crown if he's a mason. What a cheek. I don't think he'll make Commissioner of the Metropolis. Anyway, Philip, can I get you a drink?'

'Not for me, thanks. I'm sure the Chief Inspector had his reasons for asking about the freemasonry.'

'Don't tell me Rees was on the square. What lodge would have him?'

'That's not really anything I know about,' said North quietly, letting it be known that he was not 'on the level'.

Wells caught the hint and moved on. 'How can I help you?' asked the minister.

'It's a very delicate matter which is connected to the police inquiry, but it's an aspect I have been asked to look into by the Speaker, and as yet the police are unaware of it.'

'I knew you were coming with the police. They told me that you were acting for Mr Speaker in this when the appointment was made. It's a curious anachronism, isn't it . . . the Speaker having jurisdiction over a murder investigation?'

'The last murder in the Commons was Spencer Perceval in 1812. I don't think the Speaker is too keen to earn his footnote in the history books that way.'

'Nor am I. What's the delicate bit?'

'Before I get to that part, perhaps you could tell me what you know about PCW.'

'Ah . . . I see the Rees connection now. Well, there's no mystery about PCW. It was a crooked Lloyd's syndicate. A lot of underwriting members lost a lot of money and the principals involved fled to America. The corporation had tried them in their absence and levied a hefty fine for their misconduct, but they haven't been able to collect. Neither of the two culprits has returned to England but, if they did, they would be arrested at Heathrow.'

'And there are no extradition proceedings?'

'Lloyd's and the Fraud Squad have tried to get them arrested in the States but the federal courts threw out the case on a technicality.'

'And will there be a government inquiry into the affair?'

'That's what Rees wanted, amongst others of his ilk, but I have to weigh the public interest here. The decision hasn't been taken yet; that's an aspect I can't really discuss at the moment. My own private view is that an inquiry of the kind the Opposition wants would accomplish very little of a positive nature. The reputation of Lloyd's would be tarnished still further and it might undermine confidence in the City which would be a shame, given the effort it has made in recent years to clean up its act. The government is taking a strong line on City fraud but this particular case is history.'

'I'm sorry to ask, but do you have any direct or indirect interest in the decision?'

'Coming from anyone else that would be an impertinent question, Philip, but I appreciate that you are asking on behalf of the Speaker, even if I don't quite see where this is leading us. Anyway, the answer is no. I once contemplated becoming a member of Lloyd's but, to be frank, I couldn't afford it. I just didn't have sufficient assets. I'm quite pleased now because if I had joined I might have been in a difficult situation over the PCW decision.'

'Apart from a financial interest, is there any other reason why you might have a stake in which way the department's decision went?'

'I'm not sure what you're driving at, Philip. I don't know any of the people involved, if that's what you're implying. I haven't been a guest of any yachts in Gibraltar or anything of that kind.'

'Have you been placed under any pressure to come to a particular decision?'

'There are the Opposition EDMs, and all the questions Rees tabled on the matter, so that is political pressure of the most legitimate kind. I've also received confidential advice from my officials and the Attorney-General . . . and that's not for repetition, incidentally.'

'None of this is, as far as I'm concerned,' North assured the minister. 'But it has been suggested to me that improper pressure has been applied on you.'

'That's untrue and I resent it.'

'I apologise for bringing this up but it is relevant to the murder investigation.'

'I fail to see the connection.'

'I have been told that you were being blackmailed in an effort to ensure that PCW escaped a government inquiry.'

'I see. That's a very grave allegation.' Wells paled perceptibly, and chose his words with care. 'I hardly know what to say. Who has made this claim?'

'I can't say at this stage.'

'Very well.' There was a moment's hesitation. 'Who else knows of it?'

'As far as I know, there is only one other person involved, plus the alleged blackmailer.' North suspected that what he really wanted to know was whether the police were a party to this line of questioning.

'And how was Rees involved, apart from pressing for an inquiry into PCW?'

'He was told that a blackmail attempt had been made, and he was looking into it.'

'Did he believe it?'

'I don't know. He was to meet someone who was going to tell him the whole story on the night he was murdered. I gather that he thought that if you refused an inquiry into PCW he would have regarded that as prima facie evidence that you had succumbed to pressure.'

'But that's absolute nonsense,' protested Wells. 'It might merely indicate that I had considered the matter fully, and come to that conclusion without anything improper having taken place. The man must have been mad.'

'It would seem that Rees had been told enough to think that blackmail was likely.' North spoke carefully.

'And what is this blackmail, exactly?'

'It's of a sexual nature,' replied North, unwilling to have to spell it out.

The minister saved him the embarrassment. 'I can guess the rest. Is there any evidence?'

North was disconcerted by the reply. If Wells had been innocent, surely he would simply deny any involvement, he thought. 'I know of none but there is apparently a compromising videotape in existence, presumably in the hands of the blackmailer.'

'I see. Well, you ought to know that I am aware of no such videotape and no blackmailer has been in touch with me. The whole idea is preposterous and, even if an attempt was made, I would never succumb to blackmail. I'd resign instantly.'

North watched Wells carefully as he blustered, and wondered what he ought to make of the minister's performance. Several things just did not add up. He continued to speculate after assuring Wells that he gave the matter little credence and telling him that it would go no further. But there was a doubt in his mind. Wells had been dismayed by the allegation . . . but not as much as one might have expected. Furthermore, he had asked about *evidence*. Would an innocent man ask about the strength of the case against him if he was truly confident that there was no case? Perhaps Wells had done things that had left him vulnerable to blackmail . . . but an actual attempt had not been made. After all, Wells had said that he could *guess* the kind of allegation that had been made. How could he guess, unless there had been something behind it, or other, similar allegations had been made in the past? Was North just being naïve to expect a minister of the Crown readily to admit to a very junior colleague that he had indeed been guilty of an indiscretion?

North was still mulling over the implications of his encounter when he strolled through the Members' Lobby on his way back to his office. His immediate preoccupation concerned the two detectives, and what Gail Crosby had told them, if anything. Judging from the questions they had put to Wells, North thought it likely that she had opted against confiding in the police. Either that, or the detectives had thought better of confronting the minister as he had just done. This was an extraordinarily delicate matter, and he had even hesitated to pass her information on to the Speaker the previous evening. After some moments of quiet reflection North had decided that he had been duty-bound to tell the Speaker. Whether the Speaker had made the right decision was still causing him some anxiety. Nor could he be entirely sure that the Speaker had not intervened. Was that a possible explanation of Wells's surprisingly relaxed reaction to the insulting charge that he had submitted to a blackmailer? North was worried that, perhaps for what had appeared to him yesterday evening the best of reasons, Mr Speaker, perhaps unconsciously, had alerted Wells to Gail Crosby's allegations, thereby allowing him to mount a credible defence. The only problem there was that Wells's response had not inspired much confidence.

In the Members' Lobby North was handed a sheaf of telephone message slips from the message board's attendant, but his concentration was interrupted by a slight pressure on his upper arm. 'Have you a minute, dear boy?' asked a familiar voice. It was Hartley Watlingham, the smooth government whip who rejoiced in the title of Comptroller of the Royal Household but was known, behind his back, as 'Hardly Working' because of the air of effortless ease the former 10th Hussars officer exuded. In fact Watlingham's disrespectful nickname was unjustified. Although, like the two other more senior government whips, he enjoyed an exotic and misleading position in the royal household, his role was far from ceremonial. His principal duty was to write a report of the day's proceedings in the Commons for the Queen, and be received in a weekly audience at Buckingham Palace while the House was sitting. He was, in effect, the monarch's spy in the chamber.

Hartley Watlingham was also a popular figure, and had experienced no difficulty in being voted into the Whips' Office by the other whips, where the convention was that a single black ball excluded a candidate.

An invitation to join the Whips' Office was regarded as a prize indeed, the first whiff of that most addictive of stimulants, raw power. It meant access to the top and a place at the table where the important decisions of state were reached. And as well as being the fast track of advancement, it was a recognition of all the most attractive of political attributes: influence behind the scenes, where it mattered, and the ability to participate in the *real* action. He was also known as the shits' whip, for he had been assigned the onerous task, by his Chief, of handling the awkward squad, the independently minded MPs who dared defy the party whip and vote with the Opposition. Having led a squadron of Ferret armoured cars in Cyprus and Malaya, he used to

say, he had seen some dirty work in his time . . .
but nothing that compared with what went on in
the Whips' Office.

So North immediately knew that Watlingham's
friendly request concealed a demand for a chat
that could not be refused. North gestured to the
green leather bench outside the Whips' Office. 'Do
you want a word here, Hartley?' he offered.

'What about inside, for a moment?' As he spoke
Watlingham led the way into the panelled whips'
corridor. Once he was through the door North
knew that the issue was to be a serious one. For
idle chats whips sat on the bench in the Members'
Lobby, or even guided their quarry into one of
the division lobbies where they could talk in conspiratorial tones without fear of being overheard.
The main Whips' Office itself, crammed with half
a dozen desks, a fridge and two armchairs, was
occasionally the venue for meting out discipline,
but North was led further down the dimly lit
passage to the Chief's office. This was not
serious . . . but very serious.

'The Chief suggested we use his office,' said
Watlingham in explanation as he closed the communicating door to the main Whips' Office and
sat down on the leather sofa opposite the Chief
Whip's desk. 'He's at Number Twelve this afternoon and we can have a little privacy here,' he
added as North eased himself into the remaining
armchair. The room was the size of the prep
school headmaster's study and, but for the history

of the room, was unexceptional. For this had been the venue of many remarkable parliamentary scenes: where David Margesson had seen Neville Chamberlain's support melt away; where Ted Heath had held the party together after Selwyn Lloyd had lied to the Commons during the Suez crisis; where Martin Redmayne had sat up most of the night to draft Jack Profumo's fateful personal statement; where the archetypal fixer John Wakeham had advised Cecil Parkinson to find his mistress a job in Brussels. No other single room in the House held more secrets.

'How can I help you?' asked the MP innocently.

'The role of the whip is often misunderstood,' stated Watlingham gently. 'We're not here to bully and cajole, as some of our more maverick colleagues might suggest, but to help and, when the occasion arises, to offer advice.'

North shuddered inwardly. This was the standard introduction used when some highly personal matter was about to be raised. Often it involved a Member getting into financial difficulties or some embarrassing episode that was likely to reflect badly on the party. North had heard the same prologue when, a year earlier, he had been asked about the state of his marriage. Word had reached the ubiquitous whips of his discreet philandering, and it had been pointed out to him that conduct of this kind would make it difficult for his promotion. Perhaps he had intended to end the relationship, in which case no harm would have been done. North had made a non-committal answer and resigned himself to a backbench existence while Debbie was on the scene. Although his rebuke had been administered by the Deputy Chief Whip, North knew the substance of their conversation had been entered in his file, the secret dossier maintained on every Member.

'Is this more matrimonial advice?' he asked bullishly.

'Dear boy,' said Watlingham with an air of exaggerated condescension, 'this is to do with one of our colleagues. To get straight to the point I'd be interested to know why you felt the urge to seek an interview with the minister of state at the DTI.'

Half-heartedly, North made a forlorn attempt at deception. 'Export credit guarantees. I needed to . . .'

The whip shook his head vigorously. 'Won't work. The real reason.'

'The police wanted to see Roland because he was at the scene when Rees was . . . murdered.'

Watlingham gave North a quizzical look. 'Are you suggesting Roland is a murder suspect?'

'Heavens, no,' replied North, perhaps a shade too vehemently. 'That's a matter for the police. I'm there merely as the Speaker's observer.'

'Cut the crap,' Watlingham snapped. 'How deep is Roland in the shit? Don't beat about the bush. I know all the, er, ramifications . . . rent boys, injudicious friendships in the City . . . need I go on? What do the police want?'

North pondered the whip's demand. Contrary to his assertion, he quite obviously didn't know the full story, or at least the suggestion that Wells had been the victim of a honeytrap in Belfast. 'Rees had been needling Roland for an inquiry into a reinsurance fraud at Lloyd's. The police initially thought they were on the scent of some corruption and were sniffing out whether Roland had anything to hide.'

'And was there a connection?' asked Watlingham.

'None that I could detect,' North replied guardedly. 'Nor did they say anything in front of me about Roland being gay, or being involved with rent boys.' He comforted himself with the knowledge that while he had been slightly economical with the truth, the police had not delved into the minister's private life and therefore what he had disclosed to Watlingham had, in the strictest sense, been accurate. Misleading, but accurate.

'Forget what I said about rent boys,' instructed Watlingham. 'There were some rumours a while ago, and I think it was all sorted out. Don't want them reappearing, do we?' North nodded in assent. 'If anything transpires in this investigation, and I mean anything, I hope that I can rely on your good judgment to let me know, in confidence, right away. The Chief is very anxious this tragic episode does nothing to harm the party. Is that understood?'

North mumbled his agreement and fled the

room, painfully conscious that he had now committed another grave parliamentary crime . . . he had misled his whip.

North hurriedly returned to his desk in the Norman Shaw building and telephoned Rochester Row police station, anxious to know how Gail Crosby had fared in her interview with the detectives. Events were running too fast for him and he was worried that he had unintentionally burned his bridges with the whips, Mr Speaker, and perhaps even the police. But instead of being put through to the Detective Chief Inspector, he was answered by Shawcross.

'The DCI would like to see you as soon as possible, sir,' he said. 'Can you come over now?'

North agreed, and made his way out to Whitehall to catch a cab. He had a very uneasy feeling about the way events had started to turn. His sin regarding the police had been one of omission, having failed to disclose Gail Crosby's damaging comments about Wells, and North knew that Young was not the type to accept his defence, that he had been under the Speaker's instructions. The reality was that neither detective really accepted the Palace of Westminster's unique legal status. They both regarded it as an inconvenient anachronism. But what they had failed to appreciate, despite North's endeavours, was that the death of an MP, under even the most banal of circumstances, was itself an event of some consequence, at the very least for his seventy thousand electors. Whilst Shawcross had been cordial on the phone, there had been an unmistakable edge to his voice and North realised that for the first time he felt personally very vulnerable.

North's reception at Rochester Row was definitely cool, and it did not take long to discern the reason. The three men were gathered together in one of the two interview cubicles off the main incident room.

'Can you tell me how Gail Crosby was when you saw her yesterday afternoon?' asked Young.

'I've already told you. Close to the edge. Very upset but entirely rational. Perhaps a little conspiracy orientated. She was quite hostile towards me when I arrived—'

'Unannounced?' interrupted Young.

'—Unannounced. But she let me in and we had a perfectly reasonable conversation. Why do you ask? What has she told you?'

The detectives exchanged glances. 'She told us nothing. I'm afraid she was dead when we got there, and you were probably the last person to see her alive.'

North let the news sink in for a moment. No wonder they had been late for the meeting with the minister . . . and no wonder they had not been very forthcoming, not to say cool, earlier in the afternoon. Her death also explained why the detectives had failed to challenge Wells about

Gail's allegations. They didn't know . . . *and they still didn't know.* 'How did she die?'

'We've just had the preliminary report from the divisional surgeon, and it looks like an overdose. We found her curled up in a chair with a half-empty bottle of bourbon on the table. She would have known how to do a proper job.'

'What do you mean?' demanded North. This was no time to be speaking in shorthand, he thought.

'Didn't you ask her where she worked?' responded Young incredulously.

'No. I already knew that she worked for Rees as his research assistant.'

'That was only part-time. She was a pharmacist at the Gordon Hospital.'

North closed his eyes and sighed, partly in recognition of his simple error. 'I should have realised, but it never occurred to me to ask. In fact she mentioned that her fiancé had also died of an overdose . . . and that she had recognised the symptoms of his depression. If only I had spotted it. I should have challenged her when she said that. It's so obvious now . . . ' The MP paused a moment to contemplate the oversight. 'Did she leave a letter?'

'No suicide note, but plenty of ashes out in the basement garden. It looks as though she had burned a lot of papers quite recently.' North detected an element of menace in the detective's voice.

'I'm really very sorry to hear she's dead,' he said. 'She was certainly depressed when I left her, but I never considered her to be . . . at risk.'

'Don't blame yourself,' said Young, somewhat unconvincingly. 'If anyone was at fault it was us. Perhaps we ought to have gone straight round as soon as you told us about her. The trouble was, we were too involved with Toby Bellington at the time.'

To North this sounded like both an admission and an excuse. The professional investigator was acknowledging a blunder but offering a defence.

'When I spoke to her on the telephone yesterday evening to make our appointment for today she seemed perfectly all right,' said Shawcross.

So both policemen were on the defensive, thought North.

'Was there anything she said that might have a bearing on Rees's death?' Young asked, without acknowledging the truth of his inspector's statement. It was difficult to tell whether he was pleading for help or laying the groundwork for an indictment. 'Anything at all?'

'This has come as a bit of a shock,' replied North cautiously. He was very conscious that he had been manoeuvred into an awkward situation. Gail had imparted some potentially very damaging information to him, and now he was declining the opportunity to confide in the police. Worse still, he had not reported to the Speaker, which made his decision entirely unilateral. Would Mr

Speaker endorse what he had done? 'I'll have to think about that,' North concluded, non-committally.

'What we will need is a detailed statement from you describing exactly what took place. You must try and do it, however painful, while the conversation is still fresh in your mind,' Young explained. It was almost as though he was clairvoyant and had recognised the MP's dilemma . . . but he was still determined to keep a verifiable record of North's version of his encounter with Rees's mistress.

'I didn't make any notes, but I'll try and do that this evening, if you like. I have to go back to the Commons to vote.' He was keen to have another word with the Speaker before he put pen to paper and committed himself to concealing what Gail had told him about Wells. He was acutely aware that deception of this kind could end with criminal charges.

'Thank you,' replied the DCI. 'Incidentally, I'm sorry not to have been here when you telephoned earlier. I had to go straight back to St George's Square after seeing that pompous ass.'

'Do you mean Wells?' asked North curtly. It was time to put Young in his place, he thought, aware that he was under an obligation of loyalty to his parliamentary colleague to protest against the crude derision.

'Who else? I suppose we shall have to eliminate him from our list of suspects. And Gail too.'

'Was she ever a realistic suspect?' asked North, with a rather artificial air of innocence. He wanted to avoid answering Young's implied questions about Wells and Gail. He was not prepared to be pushed into a position of clearing them, only to be forced into making some difficult disclosures about them later. He opted to take the DCI at his word and accept that Gail had left no compromising letters. 'She had no obvious motive for killing Rees. They were going to get married and there was a definite financial incentive for her to stay with him.'

'That's true,' agreed Young, 'but she did have an opportunity to poison Rees and we have had no means of corroborating her claim to you of having spent the evening of the murder at home. She might have been to see Rees at the Commons . . . she could have been at the scene.'

'That's something I considered too,' admitted North, 'but there is a stumbling block. Why should she go to the Commons when Rees was anyway due to spend the night with her? It doesn't make sense.'

'Maybe so. But she had both the means and the clinical know-how to poison him. And we *don't* really know she was in her flat that night, waiting for Rees.'

'So what's the next step?' asked North.

'Neil Roberts is coming to see us on his way home. He should be here any time now.'

Chapter Eight

The Ex-Member

Neil Roberts wasted no time in establishing what he believed to be the ground rules for the interview. 'I want this clearly on the record, Detective Chief Inspector, that I have volunteered to attend this meeting of my own will. I would not wish it to be thought that I am a suspect in your murder investigation.'

'Your help is much appreciated,' said Young with a slightly obsequious tone to his voice that, North noted, had not been detected by Roberts. 'We have an appalling crime to solve and until the murderer is caught I am not really prepared to exclude anyone from my inquiries. If you feel uncomfortable about that, please feel free to consult a solicitor. But I do need your help.'

'I'm here to do what I can,' replied Roberts, backtracking. 'I see no reason to bring a lawyer into this. Just ask away.'

'First, out of curiosity, why didn't you explain who you were when we called on Mrs Rees on Tuesday?'

Roberts feigned lack of comprehension, but then answered the point. 'There was no reason. Sheila thought our relationship might be, er, misunderstood. But I was not prepared to slink into the background. Goodness knows, we have known each other long enough and I think our, er, arrangement is quite well known. Why try to conceal it?'

'Why indeed,' murmured Young as he opened a file on the desk. North guessed this was a tactic designed to intimidate the interviewee. He was unflustered, and apparently co-operative. He deserved the rattlesnake, thought North. 'Are you aware that Mrs Rees denied that you meant anything more to her than a childminder?'

'I have no idea what she said to you, Chief Inspector,' he replied glibly, as though he had rehearsed the topic. 'You'll recall I wasn't in the room during the meeting.'

'You didn't discuss it later?' pressed Young, with an air of surprise.

'Not really. She told me that you were after a hit-and-run driver and were confident of finding him. And since the papers say it was Toby Bellington, I suppose I ought to congratulate you on the speed with which you have concluded the case. He was a drunk even when I was in the House.'

'Let's be clear about this,' said Young firmly. 'Bellington has been charged with a driving offence. We are still looking for a murderer. Or murderers.'

'Plural, Chief Inspector?' said Roberts, taken aback. North could not judge whether the reaction was genuine.

'We think that Rees might have been the victim of a political assassination, or perhaps a more straightforward, old-fashioned murder made to look like an act of terrorism.' Whilst the first part of his observation sounded rather matter-of-fact, the latter remark could have been interpreted as an accusation. That's how North saw it.

'Toby Bellington was many things, but I can't picture him in the role of an urban guerrilla,' said Roberts, openly mocking the detective. It was a self-indulgent manifestation of arrogance – or a brilliant performance by a surpremely confident killer. North couldn't decide which.

'Perhaps we could turn to you for a moment, sir,' said Young evenly. Roberts had irritated him, and now he was being condescending. 'Where were you on the night in question?'

'On the night Alun died I was looking after Sheila's children. She went to the cinema and I popped over to keep an eye on them.'

'At her request?'

'Of course.'

'What time did you arrive in Lurline Gardens?'

'Shortly after seven, I suppose.'

'And when did you leave?'

'The next morning. Sheila came back around ten thirty,' answered Roberts, his voice possibly betraying a slight note of triumph, or so North thought. Roberts had effectively established an alibi for Sheila Rees and himself at the moment of Alun Rees's death. Either they were both in this together, he considered, or they were both in the clear.

'When was the last time you saw Alun Rees?' asked Shawcross. It was his turn to needle Roberts.

'I last saw him a month ago, over at the Welsh Office.' The latter comment was gratuitous, but North could see Roberts's purpose. He wanted the policemen to know that they were not dealing with some suburban has-been. Roberts was still a power, exerting influence. A man to be taken seriously. In short . . . a threat.

'What were the circumstances?' pressed Shawcross, apparently undeterred by the mention of a department of state.

'He was with a delegation of MPs seeing the secretary of state about the chemical reprocessing plant in his constituency. That's one of our babies, so I was there as an observer from the Development Agency. We said hello, but that was all.'

'What were your relations like?' asked Young. 'The encounter must have been awkward, the ex-MP and current lover in the presence of the husband . . . and his parliamentary successor.'

'We never discussed Sheila, if that's what you mean,' said Roberts, bridling at Young's explicitly personal observation. 'He had walked out on her, and we never raised the issue.'

'*He* walked out on *her*?' queried Young.

'What's so odd about that, Chief Inspector? It happens every day.'

Young made no mention of the contradiction. Others had reported that *he* had been the injured party. 'Do you know what made him do that?' he asked.

'Quite simple, really. He had found someone else. It was as amicable as these things can be. I don't know who the other woman was, but Alun had never tried to hide his philandering.'

Once again, North was suspicious. Rees's behaviour since the break-up had been a matter of common knowledge, and there had been the escapade with his secretary, but had there really been long-term affairs during the marriage? And if there had, who had known of them? Rees's answer had the ring of a well-rehearsed red herring.

'And where did you fit into this arrangement?' asked the DCI.

'Alun knew that Sheila and I had been friendly some years ago, in Wales. It was one of those things. My wife has been unwell for a long time and Sheila was lonely. One thing led to another, and we got back together again recently when she came up to London.'

'So you had not been seeing each other between the time that Alun Rees was elected, and Mrs Rees's decision to housesit for her parents while they went to Australia?'

'I don't think I would go quite that far,' said

Roberts uneasily, perhaps aware of the legal implications in telling a blatant lie. 'We kept in touch. We saw each other occasionally in London and whenever I had to go down to Wales on business.'

'Tell me about your job, Mr Roberts,' asked Young.

'It's basically relocation and inward investment. I persuade foreign companies to move to Wales. I negotiate the development grants and present a financial package that brings jobs to what would otherwise be an area of very high unemployment.'

'And did this bring you into conflict with Alun Rees again?'

'I'm not sure about your use of the word "again", Chief Inspector. I got on with Alun perfectly well.'

'But isn't it true that he took your seat, and you took his wife? Let's be blunt about this, Mr Roberts. From an outsider's point of view, you both had every reason to hate each other.'

'To the outsider, maybe. But that wasn't the case. I was set up by a bunch of Trots in the party who were determined to get rid of me because my politics were too moderate for their taste. I wasn't the only one to fail reselection. There were others too, you know. But it so happened that Alun benefited from the infighting. He didn't calculate that was how things would turn out. It was really that he was in the right place at the right time. Sheila and I were something quite different. Alun didn't bear a grudge.'

'But you were opposed to Rees over the question of the chemical company?' insisted the detective.

'That was a political issue. We had fought long and hard to get that company to move its operations to Wales. It has brought plenty of jobs to the area, and Rees wanted to send it back to Canada. We weren't going to roll over and play dead just because a few ill-informed and unrepresentative environmental activists were manipulating the media. The agency had a responsibility to take a regional perspective on this. How would it look to other prospective investors if we offered grant aid one year, and then threatened to prosecute them the next? We would have been cutting our own throats. I knew exactly what Alun was up to. He was going for short-term political popularity at the expense of long-term strategy. A lot of MPs do that. It's the price of democracy.'

'So you went to the meeting with the secretary of state to oppose Rees?'

'Not at all. The agency was represented purely in an observational capacity. We gave our advice to the Welsh Office separately. We just listened politely, took notes, but said nothing.'

'But you were utterly opposed to what he was doing?' said Shawcross, just to be certain he had understood the drift of the argument.

'Most people were. The unions wanted the jobs and I think we could have persuaded all but the most unreasonable that the processes at the site were perfectly safe and conducted within a strict, statutory framework of supervision.'

'Were *you* satisfied they were safe?' Young was both seeking a non-bureaucratic explanation, and an understanding of Roberts's own private view.

'If you are referring to Alun's television stunt, that was unpardonable. What's the point in humiliating a man who has brought employment to the place? It was shameful.'

For once, thought North, Roberts sounded sincere. But was this because he wanted to be seen to be criticising Rees for something that was patently indefensible? 'But how do you know the work undertaken there is entirely harmless?' North intervened. It seemed to him that Roberts had been rather too vehement in his support of the chemical polluter. Was he really so willing to lose whatever socialist credentials he might have had in favouring the multinational conglomerates?

'I've been there on countless occasions. I helped set it all up, years ago. You could say it's my baby. I've been in every part of that plant and I have no reason to disbelieve the Health and Safety Executive when they certify that all the correct procedures are followed. There have also been two major inquiries by the Pollution Inspectorate. The company passed those too. Alun was relying on emotion, not rational argument, to make the case for closure.'

'Do you happen to know what the by-products
are of the recycling processes?' interjected North
again, quietly.

'Various heavy metals,' replied Roberts
vaguely, even dismissively. 'They're removed
from the site and disposed of elsewhere at designated landfills that have been specially protected.
The entire procedure is reviewed and certified on
a regular basis. There's no danger.'

'And is thallium one of those compounds?'
Young asked casually.

The way he said it made the hair on North's
neck rise. The hunter was cornering his prey,
leaving few avenues for escape.

'That is the most toxic of the by-products
handled there,' Roberts conceded slowly. 'You've
certainly done your homework, Chief Inspector,
but I don't really see that Alun's opposition to the
works could have a bearing on his death.'

'Perhaps you'll leave that one to me,' Young
replied curtly, but he changed tack anyway.
'What can you tell me about Meibion Glyndwr?'

Roberts seemed relieved by the switch in direction. 'They were once a force to be reckoned with.
Nationalist extremists committed to the armed
struggle. Not taken very seriously now, apart
from a few hotheads who like to burn down cottages belonging to Birmingham businessmen.'

'Then you have no sympathy for their aims?'
asked Young disingenuously.

'You want me to support arson? Not likely.

They're very misguided in my view. I know they want to preserve the language and promote Welsh employment, both laudable pursuits in themselves, but their methods are, frankly, counter-productive as well as immoral.'

'Do you know anyone in Meibion Glyndwr?'

'That's a difficult one, Chief Inspector.' Roberts appeared to consider the question very carefully for a few moments. 'These people do not advertise their credentials. One could make a wild guess, but it would only be that . . . a guess.'

'So you have never been a member?' If North had not already known the background to Young's question he would never have noticed the subtlety that lay behind it.

'That's a very curious question,' said Roberts, in what amounted to an acknowledgment that there might be some validity to it. No righteous indignation, no exaggerated protests. 'No, I haven't. Nor has anyone else in my family as far as I know.'

'Not even in your youth?' pressed Young. This certainly sounded like a straight accusation.

He looked momentarily perplexed. 'Now I see what you are getting at. I was once a Welsh Nationalist . . . at university, you know. But that's a far cry from Meibion Glyndwr. It really is. The English have a lot of difficulty understanding this, but Plaid Cymru are utterly opposed to the extremists. As I said before, their behaviour damages the cause.'

North felt like congratulating him for wriggling neatly off the detective's hook.

'And since your last meeting at the Welsh Office, can you confirm that you never saw Rees again?' asked Young.

'Emphatically not, Chief Inspector.' Roberts had regained his confidence.

'And can you think of anyone who might have wished to kill Rees?' asked Shawcross.

'Definitely not the chemical company, if that's what you're driving at. They're quite confident of winning this particular battle. They'll use scientific evidence, not hysteria, to make their case.'

'And no political enemies that you are aware of?'

'Chief Inspector, I'm baffled by your line of questioning. I've already told you that we really had minimal contact. So what exactly *is* the relevance of all this?'

'I would prefer not to discuss that angle further, sir, at this stage. But before you go, perhaps you could give me some background on the Freemasons.'

'What makes you think I'm a mason?' asked Roberts suspiciously.

'Mr Roberts, this is a murder inquiry. Let's just say that the Metropolitan Police takes this crime very seriously, and enjoys a high clear-up rate . . . in fact one of the best in the world. We can devote almost unlimited resources to an investigation like this. And if I think there might be a Freemason connection in this crime, the Commissioner will back me. I make myself understood?'

'Perfectly, Chief Inspector. I was just a little startled by your question. Yes, I'm a Freemason. I don't really make a secret of it. At least, no more than anyone else. Alun wasn't, as far as I am aware, if that's your next question.'

'I already know, but thank you for the confirmation and your candour. It is really much appreciated, and I hope this hasn't been too much of an ordeal for you.'

Shawcross escorted Roberts out, leaving North and Young to sift through the notes they had made. 'If you don't mind me asking, was that question about him being a mason really based on the Yard's huge resources?'

Young laughed. 'In a way. It was guesswork, based on eighteen years of experience. And if that isn't the correct application of resources, I don't know what is.'

'And the thallium that killed Rees ... was Roberts the source?'

'Possibly. But it doesn't really account for how the substance was administered.'

'And what about his alibi for the time of the murder? It either implicates Sheila Rees or lets them both off the hook.'

'I fear the latter. Mrs Rees hardly fits the description of either of the two women we are seeking who were close to her husband's body, and if she and Roberts were really plotting to kill Rees I think they would have gone about it rather differently. Criminals invariably say after their arrest that they couldn't have committed a particular crime ... they wouldn't have been so stupid. But the prisons are full of unsuccessful, rather stupid criminals. The clever ones rarely get caught. But on this occasion, where there was an element of opportunism, the weight is in favour of Roberts and Mrs Rees being innocent. Together they could have planned a dozen better scenarios in which to entrap Alun Rees. In fact, we can't link either of them to the right place at the right time. We're going to have to look elsewhere.'

'This was not the news I had been expecting,' said Mr Speaker, when North brought him the latest update later the same evening. He had just passed the Chair over to his deputy, and was tired after a gruelling three-hour stint on the minutiae of the Humberside Corporation (Municipal Provisions) Bill. 'You're really no further at all ... Mrs Rees and that dreadful man Roberts are now, you tell me, excluded from the investigation, and Rees's mistress has committed suicide.'

'It doesn't look good, I agree, but the problem is that the police won't pursue the best lead, because they don't know about it.'

'I thought you said there were plenty of things for them to be looking into? Rees's secretary sounds a possibility . . . and what about her husband? Who knows, it might have been the mistress who killed him, then, filled with remorse, took her own life.'

'And how is a frightened young Canadian girl going to get Semtex explosives? Anyway, she was besotted with Rees. There's no motive, precious little opportunity. But you can't say the same about Wells.'

'You're not going to harass poor old Roland, are you?'

'I wouldn't use that word exactly, Mr Speaker, but the police don't realise Wells had a motive for murder. They regard him only as a useful witness who can identify one or both of the missing women. Their questions would have been far more hostile if they had known about this episode in Northern Ireland. But you have instructed me to protect his reputation.'

'That's not quite true, Philip,' corrected the Speaker. 'I only told you to leave the decision-making to me.'

'Surely you can't deny that the police are working in the dark? I was there when they interrogated Roland Wells and they obviously had no idea that Wells was being blackmailed, and that Rees had known all about it.'

'There you go again,' said the Speaker, feigning exhaustion. 'You don't know that Roland was being blackmailed. It's all supposition and now the wretched girlfriend is dead the matter will have to remain closed.'

'But it can't. Someone murdered Alun Rees and we have a responsibility to find the killer.'

'Dear boy, I'm not advocating we let anybody escape justice. I simply want Wells to be treated fairly. We can't go around spreading unfounded rumours about ministers of the Crown. It brings the whole House into bad odour. But there's nothing to stop you from making a few discreet inquiries about Wells if you are really determined. Just make sure you don't turn this into a witch-hunt. Men of ability in the government have a scarcity value. On second thoughts ... forget I said that.'

'So I have your permission to check out Roland Wells?'

'You have, but only if you do so discreetly. I don't want any more MPs arrested, and I don't want any more bodies.'

Once back at his office North made two calls. The first was to Rhydian Vaughan to discover what information, if any, the Opposition Chief Whip had received from the security authorities.

'Rhydian, it's Philip North. You mentioned you would ask your Chief about Alun Rees. Any luck?'

'I don't suppose it's of much use now that Toby Bellington has been charged,' he said.

'It does matter. You'll just have to take my word for it. Alun was murdered *after* he had been run down by Toby. It's a long story, so I'll spare you. The fact is that Toby has been charged with dangerous driving. He didn't cause Alun Rees's death. That was murder.'

'I see,' said Vaughan. 'My Chief was told that Alun had asked the Ministry of Defence about whether a particular soldier had served in Northern Ireland.'

'So why was the Chief involved? Surely that's the kind of routine inquiry any of us might make?'

'I agree. But this chap is on the wanted list.'

'There's a warrant out for the arrest of the man Rees was inquiring about?' North sensed he was getting close to something big.

'Yes. And it's not for unpaid parking tickets. It was the Anti-Terrorist Branch that went to see the Chief. He reminded them about parliamentary privilege, but asked me to keep an eye on Alun.'

'Have you got the soldier's name?'

'Only the surname. He's called Evans.'

North then telephoned the Commons extension for Donald Smith and found himself talking to Elaine Newman. After he had introduced himself again, he asked her to search the correspondence files on her computer for any letters addressed to a Mr Evans.

'We have about seventy. Didn't you know that everyone in Wales is called Evans?'

'How many did he write to more than once?' North was assuming his Evans might have sent more than one letter.

Elaine Newman scanned her computer's directory again. 'That cuts the figure to about twenty. Not much help.'

'Try "T",' suggested North, his mind turning back to the entry in Rees's pocket diary for the night he died.

'There are two. One in Thornhill, which is on the road to Caerphilly. The other is in London. Which "T" do you want?'

'I'll take them both. Does either strike you as the flaky SAS man?'

'Sorry. Neither rings a bell. We do get hundreds of letters a week.'

'I know, and thanks anyway.'

North knew immediately which of the two to try first. It was true that some MPs received a huge correspondence, but there was also a convention that MPs did not poach each other's constituents. If the Evans in London had been writing to Rees as an MP, for whatever reason, the honourable member for Cardiff East was under a universally recognised duty to pass him over to the appropriate MP, this one being the member for North Kensington. Theoretically, Rees should not have maintained the contact unless he had special reasons for doing so.

North was in a quandary. The London address was a pub, the Portland Arms in Portland Road. His instinct was to wait until morning, check the electoral roll and then, if the elusive Mr Evans had been listed as a resident in the pub, ask

DCI Young to interrogate him. However, North hesitated. To follow that route would mean declaring to Young how he had cottoned on to Evans in the first place. That in turn would require him to disclose his knowledge of the blackmail plot against Wells. And that, he had undertaken to the Speaker, should remain a secret for the time being. North felt trapped, partly by what he perceived as his betrayal of Young's trust, and his increasing certainty that TE and the minister held the key to what had happened to Rees. He had no doubt that Evans was the man who met Rees immediately after the last division. He was probably the last man to see Rees alive, and probably knew exactly what had occurred, and why. Suppressing the temptation to wait for the morning, North glanced at his watch. It was nearly seven o'clock. He was due to attend a dinner at the Carlton Club in an hour, but it was only a backbench dining club entertaining the Home Secretary. It was an opportunity to pose awkward questions of the kind that ministers preferred to answer in private, among friends, but now that held no thrill for North.

North walked back to the carpark under New Palace Yard and revved his Jaguar into action. He preferred not to use his car in London, but this evening was an exception. He needed to get to the Portland Arms in a hurry. He manoeuvred the car across Parliament Square, up Birdcage

Walk and then up Park Lane to Marble Arch. The next ten minutes were rather slower, as North weaved through the heavy traffic clogging Notting Hill Gate. He gave a wry smile as he passed Tony Benn's splendid house on Holland Park Avenue, and a couple of minutes later turned into Portland Road. There, straight ahead, where the road forked, he saw the Portland Arms.

North parked the Jaguar outside an architect's office and retrieved a faded denim jacket from the back seat. Removing his tie, the MP slipped off his suit jacket and pulled on the denim replacement. Moments later, he was inside the Portland Arms.

The saloon bar was noisy, filled with W11 regulars on their way home to flats in what had become a fashionable part of London. Expensive wine bars had flourished, but the Portland offered a compromise between the old-style neighbourhood pub, with a stripper on Friday night, and the leather and velvet corners installed to accommodate customers with portable telephones. North edged his way to the mock-Victorian bar and ordered two whiskies. When the barman returned with his change, North asked him where he could find Mr Evans.

'The Sarge? He'll be upstairs. Room four.' He pointed to a side door.

North nodded his thanks and carried both glasses through the door and up the dark narrow passage. There was a flight of stairs, the lino peeling off the steps. The faded décor was eloquent testimony to the limitations of the brewery budget. Plenty of brass and mahogany downstairs, but authentic tat behind the scenes. On the first floor there were several doors, and North knocked gently on Number Four.

'Who is it?' a voice called. Then, 'The door's open.'

North pushed open the door and saw a short wiry man sitting on top of a bed, his legs crossed, with a copy of the *Evening Standard* on his lap. A small black and white television was perched at the foot of the bed.

'Sergeant Evans?' asked North. 'I thought you might like a drink.' He handed the reclining figure the tumbler of Black Label.

Evans stared at him, grasping the tumbler with both hands. 'I know you, don't I? On the telly?'

'That's right. I'm Philip North. I've brought you a drink.'

'Do I look that bad? What do you want with me? Not many people call me sergeant, you know. Not any more.'

'I'm here to talk to you ... about Alun Rees.'

'Not one of those investigative reporters, are you?'

'Not exactly. I was one of Alun Rees's colleagues in the Commons. I need your help in clearing up his death.'

'All I can tell you, Mr North, is that I know absolutely nothing about it. There, that was quick, wasn't it? Hardly worth the drink, but thanks anyway.'

'But you were there?'

'I may have been there, and I was probably the last man to speak to him ... but I didn't kill him.'

'I know you didn't. But I need your help in proving who did.'

'Why should I? It'll only help the police to find me.'

'I can guarantee you won't find yourself in difficulties with the police over this. They're acting under the direction of the Speaker on this investigation, and I can assure you that you won't be arrested. It stands to reason. I knew where to find you, but I haven't brought the police with me.'

'So you say,' murmured Evans. 'How did you find me?'

'It wasn't so complicated. Rees had tried to check up on you and the Ministry of Defence had kept a record of his inquiry. Once I had your name Rees's secretary retrieved your address from her computer.'

Evans shook his head. 'Just goes to show, you can't trust a politician. Rees told me that the only record that he had kept of me was in his correspondence file, which I retrieved from him that night. And I burnt it on Wednesday, after I saw the press reports that his death had been murder. I knew I'd be in the frame for it.'

'What intrigues me is why you used your real name when you first approached him.'

'I had to, otherwise I knew he wouldn't take any notice of me. I expected him to check my bona-fides.'

'Which were?'

'D Squadron, 22nd SAS, Carrickmore and South Georgia.'

'You survived the crash, then?'

'How do you know about that?'

'My brother-in-law was in the Sea King too. He didn't make it.' Cass's brother had been killed on the Fortuna glacier, together with nineteen other members of his troop. The helicopter had crashed in appalling weather conditions during the first part of the campaign. The SAS had suffered more casualties in that single tragic incident than at any time since the invasion operations in France in 1944. North now had the measure of the man before him but, more importantly, he had established a bond between them. It was a fragile one, but Evans's initial hostility had melted.

'I knew that any MP would write me off as a crank unless I could prove my credentials.'

'And you gave him your address as well?'

'A calculated risk. I'm off back to Wales on Sunday so the police would have got no joy here. Anyway, Rees had nothing to fear from me. In fact quite the reverse. I was there to save his life. I didn't think he would put the police on to me.'

'How were you going to do that?'

'I'd rather not say, thank you. But take it from me, Rees had nothing to fear from me.'

'But you were with him when he was killed?'

'That's true. He was hit by a Mercedes right in front of me and until I heard the news on Monday evening I assumed it had been an accident. Then the police said it was murder, and now a Tory MP has been arrested for reckless driving. A drunk driver may be a murderer in the eyes of some, but I can't fathom this one out at all.'

'Rees was murdered, but after the accident. And there's another aspect to it. Meibion Glyndwr is being blamed for planting a bomb in his car.'

'I haven't read anything about that,' said Evans suspiciously.

'You probably won't. But the police are convinced there is a terrorist angle to this case.'

'And would you believe me if I assured you there wasn't?'

'That depends on you. Why don't you tell me how, and why, you contacted Rees?'

'I will, on condition this goes no further.'

'I can't give you that assurance, but at this stage I can give you the Speaker's protection.'

'And what is that worth?' asked the soldier sceptically.

'Quite a lot, especially inside the Palace of Westminster.'

'Why should I go there again?'

'Because unless you do you're not going to be

able to clear yourself of this crime. You need my help, and I think it's in your own interests to explain exactly what took place that evening. The police will have no power to arrest you inside the palace if you have the Speaker's protection. I can escort you in and out.'

'And what is it that you think I'll say that's so crucial? I only saw what everyone else saw when the car hit Rees. There were others there, you know, including a plod.'

'That in itself will be important. But I think the reason you went to see Rees has a direct bearing on this crime. Am I wrong?'

'You've got it all worked out, haven't you?' said Evans wearily. 'You really *know* that I had nothing to do with Rees's death, don't you?'

'I've never been more certain about anything. I think I know who killed Rees, but I need your story to prove it. What can you tell me about Roland Wells?'

'So you know about that too, do you? Well, that's forbidden territory. I don't want to get into all that.'

'I quite understand your reasons. What about Meibion Glyndwr then?'

'What do you want to know?'

'You're a member?'

'I am.'

'And you had a message to convey to Rees? An important message?'

'We thought so.'

'And the message was . . . ?'

'I think I ought to explain something to you first. Meibion Glyndwr is not a terrorist organisation, at least not according to most reasonable definitions. We don't kill people or maim them. Nor is this a matter of semantics for me. I've seen my fair share of body bags in my time . . . and I know about terrorism from the sharp end. The difference is, we destroy property. It's Welsh property, but it's owned by outsiders who exploit the region, push up property prices, and force our youngsters to move elsewhere. It's genocide really.'

'Hardly that,' protested North.

'I wouldn't expect you to think so, but if you came from where I was brought up, there's no other explanation. It may not be a deliberate policy, but the effect is just the same.'

'So you burn down houses.'

'Only a few. It scares off the money from the Midlands. The weekenders aren't prepared to take the risk. That reduces the pressure on the property market, and for the first time in years there are houses available that local people can afford.'

'And how did Rees fit into all this?'

'He didn't. He used Meibion Glyndwr as a vehicle for his own ambition. He condemned our activities to get personal publicity, but that actually suited us because he kept us in the headlines. That spread our message across to the very people we were aiming at: the rich incomers, the businessmen with second homes.'

'So Alun Rees was unwittingly furthering your cause.'

'Any politician willing to make a song and dance about burning down houses suited us. It's like the Mau Mau. People think that hundreds of white farmers were slaughtered in their beds and their wives raped by Jomo Kenyatta's savages. In fact there were only a handful of white farmers killed during the Emergency. What counts, though, is the *impression* left, not what actually happened.'

'And therefore Meibion Glyndwr had every reason for keeping Rees alive? Surely that wasn't your message to him?'

'No, not exactly. But we had been offered a hit. Or rather, it had been suggested to Meibion Glyndwr that Rees was dangerous, that he ought to be killed. That anyone could make such a proposition shows how very out of touch they were with our policy. We don't kill people. We never have.'

'But there was an attempt at Prince Charles's investiture at Carnaerfon?'

'That was nearly a quarter of a century ago. Don't you see? Meibion Glyndwr is feared not because of anything that has happened recently, but because of some ancient history, an incident in which two of our own men died trying to make a home-made bomb. Even on that occasion, which people always trot out to prove we kill people, there's no evidence they intended to harm anyone. They only succeeded in killing themselves, but that was long before my time.'

'How did you get involved?'

'I was invalided out of the Army after the Falklands and I tried to make a living hill-farming. It was a disaster, and I soon realised from first-hand experience how the second-homers were destroying our way of life. They ruined my only chance of making a go of things as a civilian.'

'So you joined Meibion Glyndwr?'

'They asked me whether I was prepared to do a few demolition jobs. It was exactly the kind of stuff I was trained for. Reconnaissance, clandestine infiltration, preparation of charges and covert withdrawal. I had all the skills they needed so badly. Bomb-making is not as simple as buying an anarchists' cookbook and mixing the right quantities of sodium nitrate fertiliser with sugar. It's a precision job where there's no room for error. If you do make a mistake, it's the last you'll ever make. I was taught by a professional, a real expert in his field, and I've done six houses altogether. Nobody's suffered so much as a scratch.'

'What about the contents? Didn't you think about what the owners had left inside?'

'That's bullshit, if you'll excuse me. The owners hardly went to the places I picked, which were left empty for weeks at a time. If they had left anything valuable there, they deserved to lose it. No, we selected our targets with great care. Every one was burned to the ground long before the fire brigade could reach the scene so we weren't even endangering the lives of the firemen. A lot of planning went into these operations, contrary to what the media says. This isn't mindless arson.'

'If that's the case, how do you justify Meibion Glyndwr's connections with international terrorists . . . and the Provisionals?'

'That's classic psy-ops. You really shouldn't believe your own propaganda,' laughed Evans.

'I don't understand,' said North, puzzled.

'Meibion Glyndwr doesn't have any connections with that scum. We would all have been caught by now if we had. If I saw a Provisional I'd kill him with my bare hands. They're just gangsters . . . there's nothing political about their motives. You only have to look at the fact that they're banned in the Republic. How can they be fighting for a united Ireland if the Dublin government has outlawed them? That's the difference between the Provos and the Official IRA. It's a distinction all too easily forgotten. Anyway, I can assure you that Meibion Glyndwr has no truck with the likes of the Provisionals. I think a previous generation may have had links with some of the Breton separatists, but that was a very temporary phenomenon.'

'If, as you say, the Sons of Glendower has no connection with the Provisional IRA, or any other terrorist group, where does it get its explosives from? Don't try and pretend it's ancient gelignite from Welsh quarries because the police have shown me a forensic report specifically identifying a particular bomb, the one found on Alun Rees's car, as Semtex-H.'

'On Rees's car? You do surprise me.'

'Never mind about that now. How do you explain where your Semtex comes from?'

'Where do I get it from? That's easy. The SAS.'

'Do you expect me to believe that?' North was incredulous.

'I don't really care,' shrugged Evans, 'but it's the truth. As you probably know, the regiment is based at Stirling Lines, just outside Hereford, and very close to the Welsh border. We do most of our training in Wales, on the Brecon Beacons, and occasionally we leave some of our kit behind. Sometimes it's accidental, other times deliberate. There's a hell of a stink if a piece of hardware goes missing, but with live ammunition and explosives it's almost impossible to tell how much has been legitimately expended. Suffice to say, there are one or two caches that I know about.'

'Because you planted them deliberately before you left the regiment for good, or do you just ask sympathetic friends to be careless while on exercise?'

'I don't really see that this is a fruitful area to explore. Tell me about Rees's car instead. I can't help you otherwise.'

'In a moment.' North sensed Evans's growing confidence. 'I have to be sure about this Semtex business. Are you absolutely certain the SAS uses Semtex?'

'Of course I am. It's the best plastic there is. You can shape it with your bare hands. Try doing that with regular *plastique* and you'll develop a hell of a hangover. We only used the best in the regiment. Now, tell me about the bomb in Rees's car.'

'It wasn't in, it was under. A typical terrorist device, according to the police, packed into a plastic lunchbox, complete with a mercury tilt detonator.'

'So my warning to Rees would probably have been too late.'

'Was that your message? A warning that Meibion Glyndwr had targeted his car for a bomb?'

'Haven't you listened to anything I've said?' asked the soldier wearily. 'We heard that someone was out to get Rees. That person suggested he be assassinated, which is entirely contrary to what we believe in. I was seeking to warn Rees that he had acquired a dangerous enemy . . . someone who meant business and was willing to use Meibion Glyndwr as a cover for murder. We weren't going to let that happen.'

'Wouldn't that have fulfilled one of your objectives, greater notoriety?'

'We'd get the media coverage, but we'd also get the turncoats. You can't really hide a group like

214

ours. We have political objectives and we've all been active politically at one time or another. That means we've been noticed, we're on file. We can only stay one step ahead of the Special Branch while we all share and respect the same values. Once you indulge in murder, the rules all change. Our own people, the supporters we rely on to help us, would opt out. Worse, they would be ripe for recruitment as informers. That's why the Provisionals have no hope in their cock-eyed political objectives. Most of them have been involved with Sinn Fein and are therefore well known to the security forces. But more importantly, they have alienated their own people. Their tactics have been counter-productive, and so the ranks of the Provisionals are riddled with men settling old scores by ringing in on the confidential telephone lines. What we do may ultimately hurt the shareholders of a few big insurance companies to the tune of a fraction of a penny a year off their dividend, but we don't go in for physical violence. Therefore we took the threat against Rees rather personally.'

North stayed with Evans for another hour and a half, and when they parted North was convinced that, at long last, he knew who had strangled Rees, who had poisoned him, and how a bomb had come to be placed on his car.

Chapter Nine

A Dishonourable Murder

Later that same evening North had a further session with the Speaker and, after half an hour of anxious negotiations, arranged for a special event to take place the following afternoon. Mr Speaker was going to hold a tea party, and North was to summon the guests. When North explained his plan to Detective Chief Inspector Young, he was met with incredulity.

'What on earth makes you think any of these people will come? Why should Mark Newman attend – or his wife? You'll never get Roland Wells there. And is it really wise to question Sheila Rees and Neil Roberts together? Anyway, I think Toby Bellington has gone into hiding . . . and as for your mystery man, I don't like the sound of him one bit. Where has he sprung from?'

'All in good time, Chief Inspector. The last one's my responsibility, but your task is to gather up the rest. You have the authority of the Speaker to summon them to Parliament if you so wish. You can't have any higher authority than that.

Not even the monarch can resist such a call. If you want to solve this crime, this is the only way to do it. We have already lost one suspect so we can't have any more mislaid. It's absolutely essential everyone is there together.'

'Message received, North. I only hope you're right about this.'

There were ten people in the room, a long chamber in Speaker's House. Built after the fire that destroyed almost the entire palace in 1834, its Gothic arches stretched high into the dark recesses of the gold-leafed roof. Mr Speaker had diplomatically withdrawn to his study, and his wife had absented herself. Not all of those present seemed overawed by their surroundings, so as soon as everyone had gathered North rose to his feet. He had to control events absolutely – otherwise his gamble could fail.

'I apologise for the slight deception that brought you all here,' North began, 'but Chief Inspector Young thought there was a strong likelihood that the murder of Alun Rees would never be solved unless we went through with this meeting. I have invited each of you individually, on behalf of Mr Speaker, because I know that each of you holds part of the solution to this whole affair.' North acknowledged the looks of puzzlement he received, and added, 'I know this may prove a painful experience for some of you. But this case has to be solved. And since there may be some lingering confusion regarding what happened to Alun Rees, I am authorised to tell you how he died. I'm sure you all know that he was knocked down by a car, and one of those present has been charged with that offence. But Alun did not die of the injuries he sustained as a consequence of being struck by a car. He died as result of pressure applied to the carotid artery, by someone who pretended to be giving him first aid, in full view of several witnesses. But the autopsy revealed that Alun had also accumulated a very high level of a deadly toxin. In short, if he had not been hit by a car, or his blood supply restricted by a carefully placed finger, he would almost certainly have succumbed to the poison. But in addition, if all that was not enough, his car was found to have been fitted with a bomb. In short, there seemed to be any number of different people intent on killing the same man.

'The police have not had an easy task, partly because of this, but also because of the complicating factor of where Alun was when he died. Nearly three thousand people work within the Palace of Westminster, and a high proportion of them are bound to be on duty while the House is sitting, as it was the night Alun was killed. Furthermore, Parliament is a major tourist attraction and the police have been obliged to trace literally hundreds of visitors who went through the Central Lobby that Thursday evening.

'I propose to begin by asking you, one by one, where you were at exactly ten past eleven on the night of the murder, the moment Alun Rees died. But before we begin, I'll introduce you all. From my left, we have Mrs Sheila Rees, who was Alun's wife; then Neil Roberts, his predecessor as the member for Cardiff; then Mark Newman next to his wife, Elaine, Alun's secretary. Roland Wells who will be known to you all, and Tom Evans, who will not. Beside him is Toby Bellington, Detective Inspector Shawcross, and next to me, Detective Chief Inspector Young. We will start with you, Roland, if we may.'

Wells looked nervous and his voice faltered as he spoke. 'I hardly knew the man, and what I did know, mainly through his Parliamentary Questions and EDMs, I didn't like. But that's hardly relevant. I dined in the House and voted at ten o'clock. I hung around gossiping for some time, then as I walked up the library corridor, on my way to the Members' Lobby, I bumped into Neil Roberts.' He nodded to the man who was sitting on his right, but Roberts continued to stare ahead stonily, as if he hadn't noticed. 'I thought nothing of it at the time, and then went for a prearranged television interview on College Green, scheduled for ten forty-five. I was delayed for quite a while at the barrier in the Central Lobby when I was stopped by a couple who had been dining downstairs. We exchanged pleasantries, and I accompanied them down St Stephen's Hall to St

Stephen's entrance. A second or two after we had
parted I heard a car swerve and a sickening thud.
I saw a figure on the ground, and I may have
noticed a car speeding away in the corner of my
eye . . . I'm not sure. I ran over to the body and
realised it was a colleague. I couldn't put a name
to him at first. I looked around for a
policeman . . . there's usually one on duty by the
pedestrian refuge in the middle of the road when
a division has been called, but he wasn't there.
Anyway, one arrived soon enough, and a rather
competent young woman turned up as if from
nowhere to supervise. I'm not sure, she may have
said she was a nurse . . . something like that
anyway. I stayed until the ambulance arrived,
and gave my name as a witness to the police
officer. Then, rather late, I went to do my television interview. I didn't put up much of a performance, I was still very shocked.'

'Thank you, Roland,' said North. 'Mrs Rees, you
next.'

'Well, since you are obviously going to find out
that I wasn't at the cinema, you may as well
know the truth. I had arranged to see Alun at
the Commons. It was my intention to seek a reconciliation.'

'What time did you meet him?'

'Nine thirty. I went to the family room, which
is just beyond the Central Lobby, off the Inner
Waiting Hall. We had the place to ourselves and
no one saw us. It's a rather comfortable room

reserved for the families of MPs.'

'Your lie about the cinema was not your only one, was it? You told us that you hadn't seen your husband for six months. Now why did you say that, instead of admitting that you'd been to the Commons for a reconciliation that very night?' asked Young.

'I suppose I didn't want Neil to know that I had decided to go back to my husband. That subterfuge was entirely for Neil's benefit. If Alun wasn't willing to take me, I wasn't going to mention anything to Neil and he would have been none the wiser. If it had all worked out, I was going to drop Neil. Nine thirty that evening was the only time Alun had available to see me, or so he said. I told Neil I was going to the cinema with a girlfriend and he agreed to look after the children while I was out. He often did that. Alun had mentioned that he had a dinner to go to earlier in the evening, and that someone was coming to see him straight after the division. It was an inconvenient time to see him, but he gave me no choice.'

'And what happened?'

'The usual. We had a row, and he went off to vote. Quite like old times really.'

'So he left you when, exactly?'

'At about five to ten. I then drove back to my parents' home and told Neil that I'd been to the movie. There was no reason to tell him what had really happened. It was a white lie, if you like. I

222

had to pretend not to have seen Alun for Neil's sake.'

'Did it not occur to you that Alun would make a note in his diary referring to you as "S: 9.30"?'

She shrugged. 'I hoped Neil would not find out what had happened, but I had nothing to do with Alun's death, so I had nothing very much to fear. I was long gone by the time he was run down.'

'Mrs Newman. Where were you?'

'I was in my office in Old Palace Yard. Mark had one of those boring insurance dinners to go to in the City and he was going to pick me up afterwards and drive me home. I heard the sound of the accident and I ran outside straight away to see if I could help. It wasn't the first time that there had been an accident just there. It's a real black spot. Anyway, I was one of the first there, together with Roland Wells, whom I recognised instantly. Of course, he didn't know me. At first I didn't realise it was Alun Rees lying on the ground. I tried to comfort him for a few moments, and then I saw my husband run up.'

'Why didn't you tell us this before? Was it because you thought Mark had been the driver?'

'It crossed my mind. He had been drinking heavily, and I could see he was well over the limit. I just wanted to get him away while there were so many police about. I was really in a state of shock and I wasn't thinking straight. I don't know what flashed through my head, but it was a great shock to see Rees lying injured on the pavement, and then have Mark stagger up. I wasn't thinking rationally. All I wanted was to get Mark away from the scene.'

'Your turn, Mr Newman?'

'It was just as Elaine has described. If I have to work late I often pick her up on the way home to Battersea. On this particular evening I suppose I had drunk too much at the dinner. I ought to have taken a cab, but I suppose I thought I could make it home OK. But as I came out of Parliament Square there was a tremendous commotion just ahead of me. I hadn't seen what had happened but there were people running from all directions. Usually I turn into one of the reserved spaces by St Stephen's Green, opposite Old Palace Yard, but there was no room. Instead I pulled over to the left and got out to see what was going on. A man was on the ground, and Elaine was beside him. I didn't know what had happened, and my first instinct was that she had been in an accident. Then I realised the man had been injured, and I just touched her to let her know I had arrived. She turned, got to her feet, and pulled me away. She insisted on driving home, and it was only the next day that I heard that Alun Rees had been killed. It must have happened just moments before I appeared on the scene.'

'When you heard that someone had killed Rees while he was on the ground, after the accident, what did you think?'

'I admit that it occurred to me that perhaps
Elaine had been involved. She knew I hated Rees,
and that he had been a bloody nuisance stirring
up trouble in the insurance market. You see, she
had never told Rees of my connection with the
PCW syndicate. Her life had been made a misery
by the very offensive letters and motions he had
dictated to her. She felt that to say anything was
unprofessional, and might put her job at risk.
Worse than that, she might never get another
position in Westminster if word circulated about
why she had left Rees. To be perfectly candid,
we needed the extra income. I never asked her
whether she had done anything to Rees. I suppose
I was too afraid to ask, and perhaps too ashamed
to admit that much of what had taken place that
evening was little more than a blur. I simply
couldn't remember whether Rees had been
breathing when I had appeared, and when Elaine
had hustled me away. He was unconscious, certainly, but I didn't know whether he was dead.'

'Toby?'

'I've already made a statement to the police so
I really don't see why I should go through all this
again,' he said defiantly.

'I can give you two good reasons,' said North
firmly. 'First of all, anything you say here is protected by parliamentary privilege. The police
have no power of arrest within the precincts.
Their power is derived from the Speaker and we
are all under his protection at the moment.'

225

Bellington seemed unconvinced. 'And the second reason?'

'Failure to co-operate will incur Mr Speaker's wrath and he has asked me to remind those of you who don't already know that he has a pair of cells halfway up the clock-tower to accommodate anyone who defies him.'

'Very well,' said Bellington unenthusiastically. 'After the ten o'clock division I had several drinks then I decided to drive home. I expect I hit poor old Rees and I panicked. I don't know for certain because everything that happened that night is really a bit of a haze. Somehow I got home, and I went to bed. The police claim my car was the one that hit Rees so I suppose I'm responsible. There's not much else I can say, except that it's ruined my career. My wife won't speak to me and my constituency is up in arms.'

'Mr Roberts?'

'Roland was right, of course, and I was at the Commons that evening. I had gone to buttonhole Alun and explain about my relationship with Sheila. I felt I owed him that. As an ex-Member I was entitled to go into the Members' Lobby, and I knew that Alun would be bound to be there to vote at ten o'clock. Sheila's decision to go to the cinema gave me an ideal opportunity to see him. It was quite spontaneous and, in retrospect, rather unwise. Anyway, I checked on the children and slipped out of the house and drove to the Commons. I hung around talking to old colleagues, but I never saw Alun. I had set myself a time limit so I could be back before Sheila got home. I was inside just before Sheila, but I didn't tell her that I'd popped out, or why. If I had told her, she would have been furious. Later she did ask me if I'd been out at all during the evening, and I had lied, but I could tell she had not really believed me. You see, she mistakenly thought I might have murdered Alun, and she even examined the car.'

'It's true,' Sheila Rees said. 'One of the children told me that she had come downstairs when Neil was supposed to have been baby-sitting, and although she found the television was on in the lounge, he had apparently gone out. So I knew he had lied when he had told me that he had stayed in all evening. Of course I challenged him, but he said he must have been in the downstairs toilet. I was convinced he had been involved in some way in Alun's accident, and I wanted to protect him. It was only when I heard the exact time of Alun's death that I realised he couldn't have been the driver. He and I were together at around ten thirty, and now I can understand why he lied to me.'

'Tom Evans is next,' said North. 'This is the man who had an appointment to see Alun Rees at ten thirty on the night of his death. Go ahead, Mr Evans, let's hear from you. Where were you?'

'I was with Rees at the appointed time. I met him in the Central Lobby and we walked over to his office in the Abbey Gardens.'

'At what time did you meet?'

'It must have been only just after ten thirty. Anyway, he wasn't really late. But he'd obviously had a drink before meeting me. I could smell beer on his breath. I was a bit nervous and didn't want to talk in the Central Lobby. It was much too public and there was a risk we would be overheard. It was Rees who suggested that we go to his office. He was none too keen on the Central Lobby either. On the way over I told him that he was in danger, and that someone had suggested to Meibion Glyndwr that he'd make a spectacular target. I tried to warn him that there was a genuine threat to his life, and he ought to take what I said seriously.'

'For those of you who are not aware of this organisation, it is an extremist Welsh nationalist group,' interrupted Young.

'My story must have sounded pretty feeble, looking back on it,' continued Evans. 'I couldn't identify who was responsible for wanting him out of the way. You see, I had no idea, at that stage, that Neil Roberts had been the source of that particular idea. All I could tell him was which organisation was emphatically not interested in seeing him dead: Meibion Glyndwr. Naturally Rees wanted to know how I knew, and why I was such an expert on Meibion Glyndwr and privy to their policy decisions. I started to explain, and we must have been there for about twenty minutes when we went back. Rees said he had to vote again, but I suspected he hadn't believed a word I had said, and just wanted to get rid of me. I couldn't blame him because my original story, a tale about dirty tricks in Northern Ireland, had been largely fiction.'

'Why had you made up that particular story? Rees certainly seemed to have believed it, for he told his research assistant, Gail Crosby, about it,' said North, who had noticed that Evans had not characterised all his story as having come from his imagination.

'Just to get in to see him. When I first wrote to him, I got a snotty letter from his secretary saying that parliamentary convention required him to deal only with his own constituents and, as my address was in the North Kensington constituency, he suggested that I contact my own MP. But it was Rees that I wanted to see. It was his life that was in danger, not anybody else's. So I had to think up a way of getting him to see me, even if it meant poaching in what was another MP's constituency. I tried to think of better ways, but I couldn't come up with anything. An anonymous letter would carry no weight and I didn't think my own MP could necessarily be relied upon to convey a message.' Evans paused and looked round the room.

'My solution, which I thought rather ingenious at the time, was to make up a story so sensational and, if you'll excuse me for saying so, Mr Wells, so plausible, that Rees would be bound to agree to see me. What Labour MP would have turned down such an opportunity? I spiced up my story by mentioning a City fraud and compromising a senior minister. I'm sorry, Mr Wells, but I just knew he'd see me. If I'd told him the truth about the Sons of Owen Glendower straight off, he would never have believed me. He might even have called the police. My method, though unorthodox, ensured that we could have a private meeting and I could explain that he had made a serious enemy somewhere. If he tried to check on me, I had told him just enough about my service in the SAS to whet his appetite. In fact none of it really worked out as I had planned. Rees had been bitterly disappointed when I had told him why I had really come to see him. Anyway, as we crossed the road a car came from nowhere. The file Rees had been carrying from his office went flying, and I went after it. It all happened so quickly, in such a blur, that I acted on instinct. I didn't even realise that Rees had been injured. It was only when I turned around that I saw him lying in a heap, with a policeman running towards him. I was quite nervous . . . and had good reason to be. Moments beforehand I had been talking to Rees about an assassination attempt, and now something very like it had happened with me on the scene. The police would love to build that up into a case against the Sons of Glendower. How would I explain my presence?

I didn't hang around. I split, pronto.'

'With Rees's file.'

'I didn't mean to take it, but afterwards it seemed the most sensible thing . . . to hang on to it. When I eventually read it I realised it included what there was of Rees's correspondence with me, and it might have led the police to me. I was in enough trouble already so I burnt it. But let's be clear about this. Rees was alive when I took off. A crowd was beginning to gather, and I took one look and left. There was a woman bending over him and she seemed to know what she was doing. There was a policeman there too. There was absolutely nothing I could do.'

North rose to his feet. 'Of all of you, only the Newmans, Evans and Roland Wells have told the whole, unvarnished truth. And Bellington – as much as he remembers of it. I suspect that Mrs Rees's decision to try and go back to her husband was inspired more by the news of his recent inheritance than anything else. As for Neil Roberts, he went to the Commons to kill Alun Rees and he had what he must have believed was a perfect plan. He had been mixed up with the Nationalists at university, and when he needed the Sons of Glendower he knew who to get in touch with. Neil Roberts tried to interest them in targeting Rees, but that plan was dropped because, since the time Roberts had been an activist, Meibion Glyndwr had adopted a policy of non-violence. They attacked only property, not people. Frustrated, Roberts came up with another scheme: he offered to act as a kind of mole inside the civil service, and plant a bomb in a prestige target that he knew Meibion Glyndwr would be unable to resist: the Welsh Office of Whitehall. It's actually called Gwydyr House and Roberts calculated, correctly as it turned out, that they would be bound to go for it. They entrusted him with a bomb, not realising that he really intended to kill Rees with it and make what was in reality a purely domestic murder look like a politically motivated assassination. Furthermore, Mr Roberts, you intended Meibion Glyndwr to take the blame. But how was that to be accomplished? It must have presented quite a dilemma for you. I think you stalked Alun, trying to work out a plan, and it may be that this was when Alun spotted you. He mentioned to Gail that he had detected someone following him . . . someone he thought he recognised. It was you. You had access to the Palace of Westminster and you knew how to get into the underground carpark from ground level. You had plenty of time to find Alun's car there, and had the perfect excuse if anyone challenged you. You could say that you were getting a lift home with a Member, or something equally as plausible. When you eventually found Alun's car, you fitted the bomb, and went home, only to learn that Alun had died in a hit-and-run accident.'

'It had to have been Roberts who planted the bomb,' Young explained, 'because we knew that it had been put on Rees's car while it was parked in the underground carpark. The security guards search every vehicle as a matter of routine before they go in. What we couldn't understand was how a terrorist, or someone without a creditable excuse for being in the garage, could have accomplished that, not knowing where Rees's car had been parked. One had to assume that whoever had fitted the bomb had been in plenty of time, and was prepared to spend what we estimated might be up to an hour or so searching for the car. That surely meant the bomber must have had a legitimate excuse for being there. Based on that criterion, only Palace of Westminster staff and Members really qualified. It was much later that I realised that an ex-Member could get away with it. And as for time, Roberts knew he had more than enough. He could act from the moment the children went to sleep, until their mother returned home from the cinema. He had no reason to think that in fact she was going to the Commons too, that very evening.'

'It's an ingenious explanation, I concede,' said Roberts, 'but there's no proof whatsoever. And as North has said, I had nothing to do with what actually killed Alun. I was with Sheila, at her parents' home in Wandsworth when Alun died. We both have an alibi. And anyway, what motive would I have had for wanting Alun dead? He had split up from Sheila. You heard her confirm that.'

'I think you hated Rees,' replied Young. 'He

had taken your constituency, and now that he was in the money there was a danger he might also attract Sheila back. You knew what she was like. His death would have at least two advantages for you. You'd keep Sheila, and with any luck she'd have become quite an heiress. You might also have gambled on getting a crack at fighting a by-election in your old constituency. Paul Skelly says you have been very assiduous in mending your fences locally. Those are three good motives straight away. You may both have an alibi for the moment Rees was murdered, but you definitely planted the bomb. I'm satisfied you intended to kill him.'

'Then who did strike the fatal blow?' asked Wells.

Young paused dramatically for a few moments. 'Mr North is coming to that. What confused us,' he explained 'was that we assumed that Rees had been walking *away* from the Commons when he was hit by the car. In fact he had been walking *back* to the chamber, as if for the second vote. That was a crucial miscalculation, for we think the murderer only decided to kill Rees when his wife was seen leaving the Commons. Mr North will elaborate.'

North took up the narrative. 'There is one person missing this afternoon, who holds the key to the mystery, and that is Gail Crosby, Alun Rees's mistress . . . and murderer. If Gail Crosby could be here now, she'd be recognised by at least

234

two of you: Elaine Newman and Roland Wells. She was the other woman on the pavement beside Rees when he died.'

'I don't understand,' said Elaine Newman. 'What does she have to do with this?'

'She was Rees's girlfriend, and she was there on the pavement beside you. Here's a recent photograph of her. Do you recognise her?'

Elaine Newman glanced at the picture passed to her by Shawcross, and handed it to Roland Wells. They both nodded in agreement. 'It's her,' the minister said. 'She was the one I mentioned who seemed so capable ... who took charge of the situation.'

'No wonder,' replied North. 'She worked in a hospital, and she was capable ... very capable, but very desperate. Her alibi, incidentally, was the weakest of all. She said she had been in her flat all evening, waiting for Alun Rees to come home. You see, they were living together, although they kept it very quiet and Alun maintained the fiction that he used his room in the National Union of Railwaymen's headquarters. In fact he hardly went there at all.'

'Go on,' instructed Young softly.

'I always knew Gail had poisoned Alun,' continued North, 'but I couldn't figure out her motive. Nor could I understand why she had been outside St Stephen's entrance that night. She knew that Alun had arranged a mysterious appointment after the ten o'clock division and she must have suspected that it was to be with his wife. She was nearly right, for Alun had met Sheila *before* the division, at nine thirty. Anyway, overcome with jealousy, she had decided to check for herself. Perhaps she arrived a little early, but when she reached St Stephen's entrance she must have practically bumped into Sheila. I wonder, Mrs Rees, if you recognise her too?' He handed her the picture of Gail and she examined it carefully.

'I think I probably do. I was given a rather odd look by a young woman as I left the Commons that evening. I never gave it, or her, a second thought. Seeing me must have been quite a shock for her.'

'Not so much a shock, more an unwelcome confirmation that her worst fears had been realised. She knew who Sheila was, and although Sheila probably did see Gail, she had absolutely no idea that she was Alun's mistress. Gail now knew that Alun had met his wife, but didn't know why. Her fear, that Alun was about to return to his family, or perhaps had already done so and was deceiving her, tormented her. She knew that Alun had been secretive about the person he had been due to meet after the division and here, just before ten, was Alun's wife. What more proof would she have needed to feed her insecurity? Enraged or depressed, I don't know which, Gail waited, perhaps trying to fathom out what had happened. Then when she saw Alun with Tom Evans she probably followed them to the Abbey Gardens, and waited outside to confront Alun when he was alone. But when he emerged, Evans was still with him so she trailed them back to the Commons.'

'Then, utter disaster,' said Young. 'Alun Rees was hit by a car, practically right beside Gail, and she could see that he had been badly injured. She knew that he was destined for a hospital emergency room and intensive medical attention. In that one instant she must have realised that it would inevitably be discovered that she had been poisoning him. He was in a serious condition, unconscious, and Gail knew she would be found out. If Alun managed to recover, and if the doctors told him there was poison in his system, he would be sure to know Gail was the person responsible. She was the only person with the opportunity to administer the poison. She had breakfast with him every morning . . . she told me so herself. No one else saw him regularly at any mealtime, or had the same opportunity to poison him. I expect she stole the toxin from work. As soon as I learned that she had been a pharmacist at the Gordon Hospital I knew she had murdered him,' concluded Young.

'Excuse me for asking,' said Sheila Rees, 'but couldn't Elaine Newman have given Alun the poison? Didn't she also have the opportunity?'

'Not a chance,' said North, 'although I admit I did give the proposition some thought at one stage. However, when Mrs Newman told me that she had been in the habit of making extra strong coffee for Alun every morning, I knew she must be innocent of the crime. At that time she thought Alun had been run down . . . and had no idea that poison had been involved in his death. If she had been the murderer she would never have volunteered how the poison had been administered. No, Gail was the only person in a position to poison Rees, and she realised that she was bound to be discovered. So Gail decided to finish Alun off as he lay there, for that was her sole chance of avoiding being caught,' said North. 'She had to hope that his death would be attributed to the road accident, a hit-and-run driver, so no detailed autopsy would be necessary.'

'But why should she have murdered him? If she was his mistress, as you say, didn't she love him?' asked Elaine Newman.

'I don't think she did. I think Gail realised that Alun had never loved her either. She was a convenience to him, and she was vulnerable after the loss of her fiancé. He had taken advantage of her, perhaps cruelly so, and gradually she had come to terms with the fact that he wasn't going to marry her at all. Then her love, if that's what it had been, turned to hate, and she decided to poison him, just slowly, perhaps so as to give him a chance to save himself. In fact . . . it must have looked quite likely to her that he was going to return to his wife. She had no way of knowing what had happened when Sheila had met Alun in the family room for an abortive reconciliation.'

'If this woman was poisoning Rees,' interrupted Mark Newman, 'wouldn't that fact become known after his death? Wouldn't she have expected to be a suspect anyway?'

'Not necessarily,' replied North. 'His eventual death might not have been attributed to thallium poisoning unless there was an autopsy with a toxin test. That's not an automatic procedure and I'm told there is a good chance his symptoms would be misdiagnosed as anaemia and liver failure . . . natural causes. Thallium is an extraordinarily rare toxin. Furthermore, Gail Crosby thought her relationship with Rees was well concealed. Rees, of course, had his own dubious motives for keeping her out of sight. She was stunned when I turned up on her doorstep, but I thought her reaction was the shock of having heard the news of Rees's death. In fact it was the apparent ease with which I had traced her that was more likely to have been the cause of her anxiety.

'The money must have been the last straw,' North continued. 'Here I am speculating, but imagine the scene. That was what brought Sheila Rees back to Alun, and when Gail became a murder suspect she would have used the inheritance as a compelling reason to have wanted Rees alive so she could marry him. In fact I believe she hadn't known about the money until I told her, and thereby inadvertently gave her a last chance to clear herself. She probably intended to use Alun's newfound wealth to deceive the police by pretending that she had known all about his windfall. It didn't make sense to them that she would kill Alun when a fortune was almost within her grasp. I am afraid that I unwittingly helped persuade them that Gail had really known much more about Alun's financial position than she actually did, and she also took the opportunity to exaggerate Alun's supposed fear of Sheila's psychotic behaviour. She killed Alun while appearing to nurse him. But she wasn't cradling his head. She was killing him in front of people she didn't know, and who would probably never see her again. It was only when I came to prepare a detailed account of my meeting with her that I realised what had happened.

'I was finally persuaded when I recalled that during our meeting Gail had insisted that Alun had not been unwell. But the police opinion was that anyone with the quantity of thallim he had taken would certainly have experienced loss of appetite, drowsiness and nausea. She saw him more than anyone else, but she hadn't noticed any of these things. That meant either she genuinely hadn't, which was unlikely given her medical experience and considering the fact that she had claimed to have been able to diagnose her fiancé's depressive illness, or she had lied. But proving that she had administered the poison was another matter altogether. With Elaine Newman eliminated, only Gail Crosby had the opportunity. It had to be her.'

'You can understand how her mind might have worked,' Young cut in. 'Call it her rationale. Rees might have been able to save himself if he had stayed with Gail. Instead he chose Sheila . . . or so Gail thought. Gail had wanted to make him ill, maybe to keep him away from Sheila, and then nurse him back to health. It's possible she never meant to kill him, but everything went wrong when he was knocked unconscious by Bellington's car.

'If Rees had treated her reasonably, none of this might have happened. Instead he just took advantage of her. Gail was vulnerable, and he had just moved in on her. I expect she probably wished she had understood sooner what he was like. He adored his children and for as long as Sheila was around Rees and Gail would never have had any peace. Unfortunately Gail can't be with us to give us her version of events, or take her share of the blame.

'She was close to desperation when I met her because she had heard the news that Alun's death was now being treated as a murder. Up until that moment she must have hoped that his death had been put down to the road accident, thus enabling her experiments with thallium to go undetected. But instead of the police turning up, as she had probably expected, I had knocked on her door.

'Maybe remorse for what she had done to Alun,

perhaps even the telephone call from the police making an appointment to see her the following day panicked her into taking her own life. She must have known that she had fooled me successfully ... but the police would not be so easy. They would discover that she worked at the Gordon Hospital and had access to the kind of drugs that had been administered to Alun. It was the one question I had not bothered to ask her. I knew she was his research assistant, and I had just taken it for granted that it had been her full-time occupation.'

'But without Gail Crosby's confirmation you can't really be sure of any of this, can you?' asked Roberts.

'The fact that she has now been recognised by Elaine Newman, Roland Wells and Sheila Rees is adequate proof,' replied Chief Inspector Young. 'The police sergeant on duty at the House of Lords carpark has also identified her as the first woman to reach Rees but, having established her presence at the scene, and the strong likelihood that she was responsible for poisoning Rees, we had to know why she had come to the Commons in the first place. Hence this gathering here this afternoon. Now that Mrs Rees has revealed that she too had visited her husband that evening, we can see what really happened. You are now all free to go ... all, that is, except for you, Mr Roberts. With Mr Speaker's permission I have made an appointment for you with the Anti-Terrorist

Squad at Paddington Green. Perhaps you would like to accompany me. Once we are outside the precincts of the palace I will give you a formal caution.'

As the suspects dispersed and Chief Inspector Young took a crestfallen Roberts into custody, North walked slowly back towards the chamber, through the labyrinth of corridors and courtyards that separated the Speaker's House from the rest of the Palace of Westminster. He wandered into the Members' Lobby, heading for the Vote Office to pick up an order paper with the intention of listening to the Opposition's housing debate, when he was approached by one of the political correspondents who hovered like carrion waiting to swoop down on their prey. North recognised the Sunday tabloid's lobby correspondent on an interception course. He was a sharp, bearded man with a reputation for being well informed, and for being the principal contributor to an anonymous diary column which retailed much of Westminster's more tantalising gossip.

'Can I have a word, Phil?' asked the journalist. It was a request that was rarely refused, for a discourteous brush-off would be likely to result in a mention in his annual list of 'useless MPs'.

'Not another sex-change vicar committing suicide in my constituency, I hope,' mocked North.

'A bit closer to home, I'm afraid. I've had a whisper about a minister resigning ... something to do with this business over Alun Rees.

Could it be some of his departmental colleagues are not too happy with his performance? Heard anything about it in the tearoom?'

North hesitated a moment to consider his response. He knew from experience that the only way to kill an unhelpful newspaper story was to offer the reptile concerned an even sexier one. The news of Neil Roberts's arrest would be announced shortly by Scotland Yard and that seemed far more palatable than a sordid item about the murky affairs of a junior minister. 'Sounds a bit iffy to me, Bob,' replied North, thereby undermining his confidence in his piece, 'but I can tell you that the police have wrapped up the case and made an arrest.'

'Christ,' muttered the correspondent as he fumbled for his notebook. 'Any idea who it is?'

'Off the record?' asked North unnecessarily. Any attribution of a remark within the lobby would be a breach of the Press Lobby rules, regarded as a heinous offence.

'Yeah, strictly lobby terms. No one will know it was you who tipped me off,' reassured the journalist earnestly. 'So who is it?'

'Neil Roberts,' said North conspiratorially. 'He was Alun Rees's predecessor in his Cardiff seat.'

'Holy shit,' cursed the hack with enthusiasm. 'That's great. The picture desk will be bound to have him on file.' He was thinking aloud. 'I must get the cuts out quickly. This is terrific.' The journalist turned on his heels and was about to depart when he swung around to face North. He looked at him suspiciously. 'So how do you know all this? What's your involvement?'

North grinned mischievously. 'That,' he replied loftily, 'you will never know. My lips are sealed.'

More Enthralling Fiction from Headline:

FLOATING VOTER

AN ENTERTAINMENT

JULIAN CRITCHLEY

'Whitehall's pre-eminent farceur' *Guardian*

'Julian Critchley is the Peter Ustinov of politics...fluent, fluid, flinty and flammable' Julie Burchill, *The Sunday Times*

'A delightful, nonsensical scamper across the party conference' Charles Kennedy, *The Scotsman*

While the Tories might not actively welcome women into Parliament, actually killing a woman with political ambitions is going rather too far – particularly if it takes place in Brighton when the Tory conference is in full swing. But while the Party elite concentrate on who has been invited to the Jeffrey Archer party, someone *is* contemplating murder most foul.

Joshua Morris – MP, amateur sleuth, and Chairman of the Sherlock Holmes Society of Great Britain – quickly discovers that many people might have wanted to murder the gorgeous, ambitious Amaranth Wilikins.

Could it have been Sir Ralph Grunte, whose party less-than-faithful were trying to unseat and replace him with Amaranth, or his over-loyal sidekick, ex-bruiser Leroy Burns? Or had Charles Harvey, sleek junior minister, found her too hot to handle? Just what had she known about David Swan, the former Mayor of Arden? And then there was the media; how far would TV interviewer Hyacinth Scragg go to increase her ratings or sleazy journalist Ron Barton to get off a sexual assault charge? Not to mention the Government itself – could someone have misconstrued the Prime Minister's innocent but indiscreet comment about Amaranth's disposal...?

'Wickedly funny' *Independent on Sunday*

'A delicious lampoon' *Sunday Telegraph*

'Very enjoyable' Moira Shearer, *Daily Telegraph*

Don't miss Julian Critchley's first irresistible concoction of murder, politics and gossip, *Hung Parliament*, also available from Headline: 'Will tickle Parliament apart' *Daily Mail* ; 'A gloriously scabrous romp by an insider that strips the Mother of Parliament down to her knickers' *Good Book Guide*; 'Salacious' J Enoch Powell; 'Sexist' Mo Mowlem, MP; 'Deliciously waspish' *The Times*; 'Captivated me' Lord Wyatt; 'A triumph' Austin Mitchell, MP

FICTION/CRIME   0 7472 3987 8

More Crime Fiction from Headline:

JANET LAURENCE
A DEEPE COFFYN

A DELICIOUS CONCOCTION OF CRIME AND CUISINE

The Society of Historical Gastronomes is gathering for a weekend symposium on food from the past. Darina Lisle has been asked to cater for the occasion and has prepared a multitude of exquisite dishes – from salmagundis to a deepe coffyn – culled from ancient recipe books.

But when the chairman is found stabbed to death with a boning knife, the professional pique of the attendant foodies takes on a more sinister meaning. Discarded lovers, jealous colleagues and a plagiarised author have good reason to resent the victim's success. Darina, too, is under suspicion and determines to clear her name by revealing the murderer's true identity.

'Darina's debut performance is immediately appealing; she should return soon'
Financial Times

Don t miss Janet Laurence's A TASTY WAY TO DIE and HOTEL MORGUE, featuring Darina Lisle and available from Headline:
'Filled with mouth-watering recipes as well as mystery' *Sunday Express*

FICTION/CRIME 0 7472 3772 7

A selection of bestsellers
from Headline

THE CAT WHO WASN'T THERE	Lilian Jackson Braun	£4.50 □
THE SNARES OF DEATH	Kate Charles	£4.99 □
THE POISONED CHALICE	Michael Clynes	£4.50 □
MURDER WEARS A COWL	P C Doherty	£4.50 □
COLD IN THE EARTH	Anne Granger	£4.99 □
MURDER MOST HOLY	Paul Harding	£4.50 □
RECIPE FOR DEATH	Janet Laurence	£4.50 □
MURDER UNDER THE KISSING BOUGH	Amy Myers	£4.99 □
A FATAL END	Ann Quinton	£4.99 □
FATAL FEVER	C F Roe	£4.50 □
DYING CHEEK TO CHEEK	Diane K Shah	£4.99 □

All Headline books are available at your local bookshop or newsagent, or can be ordered direct from the publisher. Just tick the titles you want and fill in the form below. Prices and availability subject to change without notice.

Headline Book Publishing PLC, Cash Sales Department, Bookpoint, 39 Milton Park, Abingdon, OXON, OX14 4TD, UK. If you have a credit card you may order by telephone — 0235 831700.

Please enclose a cheque or postal order made payable to Bookpoint Ltd to the value of the cover price and allow the following for postage and packing:
UK & BFPO: £1.00 for the first book, 50p for the second book and 30p for each additional book ordered up to a maximum charge of £3.00.
OVERSEAS & EIRE: £2.00 for the first book, £1.00 for the second book and 50p for each additional book.

Name ....

Address ....

....

....

If you would prefer to pay by credit card, please complete:
Please debit my Visa/Access/Diner's Card/American Express (delete as applicable) card no:

Signature ....Expiry Date ....